"So your parents met _____ said with an odd look on his face.

"Well, so to speak. They actually saw each other once before in Forsyth."

"You and I met here, too, you know," he said. "I think you've forgotten."

"Here?" She searched her memories. "No, Jim. We met at Abby and Rafe's wedding, remember?"

"Think back, Addy. Remember the day Abby came to apply for the temporary job for her band? Because the Lynch girls were going away on vacation?"

Suddenly light broke through the darkness. She remembered following Abby into the little office. Rafe had been there, and. . .Jim! He was the one who took Abby's application. "Yes, I do remember now. I was in such a hurry to get away from the place, I couldn't think of anything else. I just knew Abby would try to talk me into entering the cave."

"You were wearing a blue dress with lace on the sleeves and collar," he said. "And you had a blue ribbon in your hair."

"Fancy you remembering that." How could he have carried around such a momentary memory for all this time? Even to remembering what she was wearing?

"It was easy for me to remember, Addy. You were and still are the most beautiful girl I've ever seen."

FRANCES DEVINE grew up in the great state of Texas, where she wrote her first story at the age of nine. She moved to Southwest Missouri more than twenty years ago and fell in love with the hills, the fall colors, and Silver Dollar City. Frances has always loved to read, especially cozy mysteries, and considers herself blessed to have the opportunity to write in her favorite genre. She is the mother of seven adult children and has fourteen wonderful grandchildren. For more information, visit her blog at www.francesdevine.blogspot.com.

Books by Frances Devine

HEARTSONG PRESENTS
HP847—A Girl Like That
HP871—Once a Thief
HP891—Sugar and Spice
HP955—White River Dreams
HP972—White River Song

White River Sunrise

Frances Devine

Heartsong Presents

I dedicate this book to Eldon and Angie Shivers who helped me to find my love for Silver Dollar City. Thank you for taking me there at Christmas time and for all the fun times thereafter. To Torey Shivers, another SDC buddy, thanks for sharing your family fun days with me. And to all of you who love not only Silver Dollar City, but the scenery, the atmosphere, and the soul of the area, I hope I've captured just a tiny bit of the wonder of it all. May God bless you with many more years of enjoyment at Silver Dollar City.

A note from the Author:
I love to hear from my readers! You may correspond with me by writing:

Frances Devine
Author Relations
PO Box 721
Uhrichsville, OH 44683

ISBN 978-1-61626-592-2

eBook Editions:
Adobe Digital Edition (.epub) 978-1-60742-710-0
Kindle and MobiPocket Edition (.prc) 978-1-60742-711-7

WHITE RIVER SUNRISE

All Scripture quotations are taken from the King James Version of the Bible.

This book is a work of fiction. Names, characters, places, and incidents are either products of the author's imagination or used fictitiously.

Our mission is to publish and distribute inspirational products offering exceptional value and biblical encouragement to the masses.

PRINTED IN THE U.S.A.

prologue

She stood on the bottom step of the train for a moment and looked at the old depot. Nostalgia rushed over her. Hard to believe it had been fifty-five years since the first train had pulled into this station.

Ignoring Paul's hand, Addy stepped down from the train unassisted onto Branson's busy platform. Her grandson had offered to fly her here, but at seventy-nine, she didn't welcome new adventures. Her stomach jumped. Except for this one. This was one adventure she would not miss.

Paul's hand cupped her elbow. "Grams, they're waiting."

A long, black limousine stood at the curb. Tomas, his salt-and-pepper hair slicked back, stood by the door attempting to hide a grin.

Why everyone thought it was amusing for her to be here was beyond her comprehension.

"Hello, Tomas. How is your arthritis these days?" There. That should take him down a peg or two.

Instead his grin widened. "I think it's some better, ma'am." He opened the door with a flourish, and she slid onto the deep leather seat.

She tried not to gawk as the car slid smoothly and noiselessly down the street, past building after unfamiliar building. Was nothing the same? Her heart fluttered at the sign that said MERCANTILE. She shook her head at her foolishness. Of course it wasn't the same one. Why had she imagined it would be?

They stopped at a light, and Addy stared at a building under construction. A sign said SKAGGS HOSPITAL. "I thought Skaggs Hospital had been here awhile."

"Yes, ma'am." Tomas's hat bobbed. "They're adding on to it. Going to be a fine medical facility when it's all done."

"Are we going to the hotel first?" She had freshened up on the train and was eager to see the downtown area.

"No, ma'am. Not enough time," Tomas said. "They told me to bring you right on over. They don't want you to miss the grand opening."

She pushed down a tinge of disappointment. She hadn't been back since her beloved sister Abby passed away back in '51. The familiar tug of grief tightened her chest, and she took a deep breath. Abby wouldn't want her to be sad today.

Even in the fifties, there had been changes. A lot of them. Ah well, she could see the town later. And maybe visit the old farm.

Addy perked up as they turned onto a familiar dirt road. The way to Marble Cave. Or Marvel Cave as they called it now. Excitement stabbed at her. Of course she couldn't miss the opening. A new craft park. But more than a park. Or so they'd told her. Built on the land where the old mining town of Marmoros used to stand, just above Marble Cave. And her husband would be waiting to escort her through the frontier-style town. Silver Dollar City they called it, although she had no idea why. She chuckled. There was about as much chance of finding silver here as there'd been of finding marble in the cave. Still, it was a nice name.

"What's so funny, Grams?" Paul smiled and laid his hand on hers.

Her heart squeezed. She loved this boy so much. Just twenty. Youngest son of her eldest son, Jack, who they'd named after her pa. That is, her second pa. How sad she seldom thought of the first one. "I was thinking how some things change so much and others are always the same."

"Look. There's Grandpa and Dad and Uncle Rafe." He leaned forward, eager as always to join the men of the family.

"Oh, Great-Aunt Betty's standing right behind them."

She squinted against the brightness of the sun until she made out the form of her husband. The car pulled up in front of the big wooden gate. He stepped forward and opened the door. They reached for each other at the same moment, and their hands touched. His eyes crinkled, and creases deepened in his wrinkled face. Wrinkled, but still handsome after all these years.

As she stepped out of the car, he leaned over and brushed a kiss across her lips. He whispered in her ear, "You're going to love it, sweetheart. And I have a surprise for you."

A jolt of excitement thrilled her. Her darling knew how she loved surprises.

Betty shoved her way in and threw her arms around Addy. "I'm so glad you're here, sister. It's been too long."

Addy laughed. Her younger sister had just visited them at Christmas. "Yes, it has been. And I'm glad I'm here, too."

Her husband placed a protective arm around her shoulders and guided her toward the gate.

"Hello, Mom." Jack planted a kiss on her cheek and smiled. "How was your train ride?"

"Fun. It was fun." She grinned. "I still love trains."

"Hi, Addy."

Tears filled her eyes as she hugged her brother-in-law, Rafe. The sight of him brought back a vision of her twin sister.

"Tuck would have loved this," he said.

Addy nodded and turned away. Rafe was right. Abby should be walking by her side, her head thrown back in joyous laughter. The thought was almost more than Addy could bear.

She glanced around. Oak trees stood on all sides, just like they had when Marmoros still stood. Addy could almost imagine the charred smell of the burned-out town. But of course, that was silly. She shivered, and her husband pulled her closer as they walked through the gate.

one

Branson Town, May 1905

"Sam Thornton! I see you back there. Turn loose of Amanda's hair right now." Addy Sullivan frowned at the nine-year-old culprit who dropped the braid and tried to look innocent. Another few seconds and the blond strands would have been saturated with ink.

Amanda's screech reverberated through the room, piercing Addy's temples. The girl glared at Sam. "You leave me alone."

"Aw, I wasn't really gonna do it." Sam's face flamed as giggles and guffaws burst out across the room.

"Children, that's enough." Addy walked to Amanda's desk and examined the long, neat braid just to make sure damage hadn't already been done. She patted the girl on the shoulder and then returned to her own desk.

Lifting the small filigreed watch that hung from a black ribbon around her neck, she breathed a sigh of relief. Ten more minutes and it would be time to ring the bell. "Children, make sure you have copied all the homework assignments that are on the blackboard. And don't forget, your essays are due on Monday."

A corporate groan rolled across the room, and Addy hid a smile. Smug expressions on several faces revealed the ones who had not procrastinated. The others would have to scurry to get them done over the weekend.

A memory popped into her mind, the picture of her sister Abby, her face pale, hand stretched out, waiting for a ruler to descend. The sound of the ruler slapping against her sister's tender palm remained with Addy to this day. After that incident, Addy had always made sure her sister's assignments were on time, even if she had to do them herself.

"On second thought, I'm going to extend the date to Wednesday. I expect every essay to be complete at that time."

Probably not fair to the ones who'd done their work on schedule and maybe it sent the wrong message to those who hadn't. She took a deep breath. Everyone needed a little mercy now and then.

She rang the bell, and the students filed quietly out. Seconds later, hoots of joy sailed back through the door. Addy grinned as she straightened the room and gathered her things together. She couldn't say she loved teaching, but the children made her heart sing when they weren't making her head pound. She locked the door behind her and went outside.

Twelve-year-old Bobby had just arrived from the livery stable with her horse and buggy. He petted the dappled mare, a gift from Rafe and Abby when she'd started teaching.

"Thank you, Bobby." She took the reins and gave him a coin.

"It warn't nothin', Miss Addy." He tossed the coin up and caught it then headed back toward the livery.

Addy bit her lip as Bobby walked away. He'd been faithful and eager to attend school last year and made wonderful progress but hadn't come back when school started. The child had to help his mother keep food on the table. Everyone knew his father had deserted the family over the summer. She blinked back angry tears. How could anyone walk out on a family?

Longing washed over her. She'd been lonely when Abby got married and left home. A part of her was missing, and she had no idea what to do about it.

Ma, sensing her discontent, had suggested she get her teaching certificate and be ready to accept a teaching position when one came available. This past year she'd been fairly content. But lately, whenever her eyes would rest on Abby's twin toddler boys, David and Dawson, the old empty feeling returned.

The sound of footsteps drew her attention. A tall man walked briskly toward the schoolyard from the direction of the stable. A lock of dark hair fell across his forehead, and gold-flecked brown eyes sparkled when his glance fell upon her. He stopped a few steps before he reached her and gave her a slow smile.

She gasped, then with a toss of her head, turned her back on him and climbed into her buggy. When she looked up, he gave her a puzzled look, tipped his hat, and walked away toward the new Branson Hotel.

Her heart pounded as she urged her horse toward home. The very idea. What impudence from a total stranger. If she hadn't turned away, he would doubtless have spoken to her. She really should talk to the school board about fencing the schoolyard, so people wouldn't use it as a shortcut to the main part of town.

But the man's handsome face—and there was no denying he was handsome—remained with her as she turned onto the lane leading to the Sullivan farm. A niggling worry pinched at her. Now that she thought about it, that face seemed rather familiar. Oh dear, what if he was one of Papa's acquaintances? Or perhaps he was connected with the new school board in some way. Now that Branson had an official school district, things weren't as casual as they had been when she was hired for the teaching position. She racked her brain for a clue to his identity. She must be mistaken. There were so many new men in town connected with the railroad. She'd probably seen him around town. That must be it.

She drove to the barn, and after she'd unhitched the horse, she went to the house. The smell of fried chicken permeated the air. Her stomach growled in anticipation as she headed to the kitchen.

"Addy, Addy." Her three-year-old sister grabbed her around the legs and hugged.

She bent down and kissed the plump cheek.

Betty's blue eyes twinkled, and she whispered, "Mama made fried chicken."

"Oh I know. My tummy is rumbling just from the smell." She grinned. She'd enjoyed that fried chicken since Ma Lexie and Papa Jack had adopted her and Abby when they were eight years old.

Betty giggled and skipped off.

Ma was placing a pan of biscuits in the oven. She straightened and turned. "Addy, you're home. How was your day?"

"Tiring. How was yours, Ma?" She gave Ma a kiss on the cheek. "I'll go change and set the table."

"All right. Don't forget to set extras. Abigail and Rafe and the twins are coming for supper, remember?" A dreamy look crossed her face, as it always did when she spoke of her grandsons.

Addy could understand that. Every time she saw her little nephews she wanted to squeeze them tightly.

"Oh by the way, did you happen to run into Jim Castle today? He's back in town, you know."

Addy stopped short on her way to her room. Her mouth flew open. Jim Castle? No wonder he'd looked familiar. He must either think she was a total idiot or very ill mannered. Embarrassment washed over her. How could she not have recognized her brother-in-law's good friend and best man?

❧

Addy Sullivan! Still as beautiful as ever, and no ring that Jim could see. Of course, he could have missed it, during the short minute before she turned her back on him. He could kick himself for gawking. No wonder she took off so fast. Still, he'd have thought she'd at least have said hello. After all, he and Rafe were good friends.

He sat in the conference room of the Branson Hotel and let his thoughts wander as Charles Fullbright, the representative for Branson Town Company, discussed the benefits of the new hotel with potential future businessmen.

Tourism in the area was already starting to flourish, with Marble Cave and the float trips every summer. Now with plans for the Maine Exhibition Building from the World's Fair to be moved here and reconstructed as a hunting and fishing lodge, adventure-seeking men would flock to the area. And this new luxury hotel would draw their families.

Jim predicted that once the White River Line began passenger service next month, tourism would triple. He calculated Fullbright would need his services here in Branson Town for at least a year. Twelve months to get better acquainted with a certain blond beauty. Maybe he could finagle a meeting at Rafe's house.

He grinned. As much as the girls looked alike, when he'd first seen them that day at Marble Cave more than three years ago, he'd been instantly drawn to Addy rather than her outgoing twin. But for some reason, he and Rafe had gotten their wires crossed, Jim thinking Rafe was in love with Addy while Rafe thought Jim was interested in Abby. When they'd finally figured it out, they both felt foolish but mostly relieved that they wouldn't be competing for the same girl's affections.

Well, Rafe got his girl. They'd been happily married for three years and were the proud parents of eighteen-month-old boys. Jim heaved a deep breath. Rafe was a local farmer and doing well. He'd built a home on land his pa had given him. Steady and reliable, that was Rafe.

Jim, on the other hand, was never in one place for long. How could he ask a woman to share his life? What woman in her right mind would agree to travel all over the country? Not Addy, he was sure, as close as she was to her twin. Not even if, by some miracle, she fell in love with him.

A burst of laughter invaded his thoughts, and one of the prospective hunting lodge owners boomed out. "At least we don't have to do business in a town called Lucia."

One of his partners laughed. "I would never have opened a hunting lodge in Lucia."

Fullbright smiled. "Well then, men, it's a good thing that Branson Town Company managed to purchase the Lucia post office and land and choose the name we preferred for the town."

"And what the people of the area preferred from what I hear," another booming voice input.

Irritation bit at Jim. "That's right, they did. But the original owner was a good man. I'm sure he had his reasons for choosing the name of Lucia and for not wanting to sell. After his death, his sons honored his wishes as long as they could."

The room quieted, and some of the men threw curious looks his way.

"Well, gentlemen"—Fullbright stood—"I believe we've covered everything on the agenda for the present. Castle and I will be available for consultation if any problems or concerns should occur to you."

The men filed out, leaving Jim and Charles Fullbright in the room. Fullbright peered at him through narrowed eyes. "What was that all about?"

Jim shrugged. "Nothing really. Thomas Berry was a veteran and a good man. He and his entire family were hard workers. I guess I'd just like him remembered that way."

"So you knew him personally?" Fullbright peered at him, his eyes scanning his face.

"No, but his neighbors thought a lot of him. They got a little edgy when he balked about selling the post office to the railroad, but they didn't seem to lose their respect for the man. I guess they figured he had a right to do what he liked with his own property." Jim put his hat on and nodded. "Guess I'll be on my way if you don't need me."

"No, no, that's fine. But Castle, don't be riling up these businessmen. We plan to start selling off lots to the locals for businesses in the next few months. That's how Branson Town will be built up, you know."

"I know. I'll keep that in mind. Don't worry, I won't upset the apple cart." He nodded again and left then stood outside the hotel.

A boardwalk lined the dusty street. Not much, but an improvement over three years ago. Two saloons stood opposite each other as though squaring off for a duel. And a small hotel stood around the corner, overrun with the railroad workers who had been pouring in. Plenty of business for both hotels. And as more and more workers filled the town, it wouldn't be long before the Branson Hotel would be full as well, even though its prices were higher.

He envisioned a town with respectable businesses lining the street. Businesses that could service not only the tourists that flocked to see the sights but also the many families moving to the area. Cafés, barber shops, maybe a ladies' boutique or two, and a hardware store.

He shook his head. Why should it matter to him what sort of town grew from this small beginning? Rafe and Abby mattered of course, but as long as the tourism drew people, there would be revenue for the railroad, and it would also benefit the locals. It always did.

A vision of Addy's thick blond curls hit him like a locomotive. She'd marry and have a family some day. Who would the lucky man be? For a moment he entertained a picture of Addy by his side as they walked hand in hand down a street of neat businesses and homes with picket fences encasing neat lawns and shrubs standing like sentinels in front of wide porches.

Realizing he'd been holding his breath, he let it out with a loud *whoosh*. He had to stop this foolish daydreaming. He was behaving like some love-struck girl instead of a man with a purpose in life.

two

Perspiration poured down Reverend Smith's face as he pounded the pulpit. A giggle, followed by a sharp slap, resounded from somewhere off to the side of the building.

Addy winced. Why couldn't people correct their children in private? She sighed. At least they had children to correct.

No, she wouldn't go there. Most of the eligible bachelors had been snapped up, and she'd turned several of them down anyway, including Reverend Smith, who'd married Carrie Sue Anderson six months later. But that was fine with Addy. None of them had moved her heart, and she wasn't about to marry unless she was in love. And with a man who loved her, too.

A picture of deep-brown eyes and dark, wavy hair crossed her mind, and she drew in a sharp breath. She darted a glance around to see if anyone had heard. Now why had she thought of Jim Castle? Especially in the house of God. Drawing herself up, she focused on the preacher, who now spoke calmly about accepting God's will for one's life and avoiding the temptation to do things one's own way.

Lord, are You telling me it's not Your will for me to marry? I want Your will for my life more than I want anything else, but— A pang of guilt shot through her. If it really was God's will for her to remain single, there could be no "buts."

A few minutes later, the reverend closed in prayer, and one of the deacons led the congregation in a final song.

Addy headed for the door, and after she shook hands with Reverend Smith and Carrie Sue, she glanced around for Ma and Pa. She spotted Abby motioning from her and Rafe's wagon and walked over.

"Addy, come to dinner. I have a humongous pan of fried chicken warming in the oven, and we need someone to help us eat it."

"I don't know. I have papers to grade." She reached over and tickled little Dawson under the chin and was rewarded with a giggle. She'd much rather spend the afternoon with her sister and nephews than grade papers.

Abby waved her hand in the air and grabbed for Dawson, who nearly slid off her lap. "Oh, do it later. I promise we'll get you home early."

"Well, all right. Let me tell Ma and Pa to go on without me."

"I already did. They left five minutes ago." Abby grinned, patting the seat beside her. "C'mon, I'm driving."

Laughing, Addy climbed up next to her then took Dawson onto her lap. "So that's why Rafe and Davy are in the back. You knew I'd have to say yes or walk home."

"Tuck always has a plan," Rafe said with a laugh. He was the only one who still called her sister by the nickname she loved. Short for Kentucky, where they'd lived until they were four. Shortly after their mother died, their pa had moved them to the Ozarks—lock, stock, and barrel as he called it. A few years later, he was gone, too.

Addy shoved the memories away and bounced Dawson on her knees while she and Abby laughed and talked all the way to the Collins' farm.

The first view of her sister's home always took Addy's breath away. The small frame house nestled at the foot of a flower-covered hill. A myriad of red, purple, white, and blue blossoms spread like a giant bouquet from the top of the gentle slope down to the edge of Abby's backyard. A fence peeked out from behind the house. It protected Abby's vegetable garden from critters. A henhouse stood beside the barn. Guineas waddled around freely, occasionally taking off in flight and perching on tree branches. A short distance away, a tiny stream danced over rocks as it rippled its way to the nearby White River. She wondered if the trains from the new railway would interrupt the tranquility that reigned here.

Abby climbed down and came around to take Dawson from Addy's arms. She set him down, and he wobbled over to his brother.

"I love your home." Addy hoped she didn't sound as wistful as she felt.

"Thanks, sis. So do I. Every day I thank God that Rafe's father and mother were generous enough to deed this section of land over to Rafe. A lot of young couples aren't as blessed."

She took little David's tiny hand in hers and helped him toddle along, while Rafe did the same for Dawson.

Addy caught her breath at the tender smile that passed between her sister and brother-in-law. It never ceased to amaze her how her independent, tomboy sister had taken to marriage like a duck on a June bug. Not that she had changed that much. But she'd mellowed. Addy grinned. That was an expression they used when people got older, and Abby most definitely was not old in any way.

She followed them inside and, as soon as she stepped through the door, felt a tug on her skirt. David gazed up at her, a sweet smile on his face, then lifted his arms. Laughing, she picked him up. "All right, Davy boy. You know Auntie Addy will do anything you ask."

The words were hardly out of her mouth before he squirmed to get down. She set him gently on the floor and followed her sister to the large, comfortable kitchen. Wonderful aromas tantalized her senses.

"Let me wash my hands, and I'll set the table for you." She went to the wash basin that sat on a table in the corner. A moment later, she took dishes out of the cupboard and began to place them on the long table.

"Thanks, sis." Abby fluttered around the kitchen, getting

things ready. "Oh, set an extra plate. We have another guest coming."

"Who?" Her stomach jumped. She knew exactly who.

Abby threw an innocent look her way. "Do you remember Rafe's friend, Jim Castle?"

"Yes, of course I remember Mr. Castle. He was Rafe's best man, wasn't he?" Oh dear. Had he mentioned to Rafe that she hadn't recognized him when he'd approached her in town? Or worse still, did he think she'd just been flat-out rude?

"There's a horse coming up the lane. That must be him now." Abby grabbed a thick cloth and opened the oven door then pulled out the pan of fried chicken.

A tap on the door was followed by Rafe's voice welcoming his guest.

Addy groaned. How was she going to face him?

☙

Jim lifted a drumstick and bit into its salty, crunchy goodness. His glance drifted across the table where Addy sat staring intently at her plate. He put the chicken leg down and cleared his throat.

She jerked her head up and met his glance then quickly brought a forkful of potatoes to her lips.

Okay, now he'd embarrassed her. He wasn't sure how, but he'd try to rectify it. "Mrs. Collins, I believe this is the best fried chicken I've ever had."

"Thanks, Jim, but why are you calling me Mrs. Collins? Did you all of a sudden forget my first name?"

"Okay then, Abby, I believe this is the best fried chicken I've ever had."

"Thanks, but you should taste Addy's." She sent an amused smile in her sister's direction. Jim wasn't sure what was so amusing, but she was obviously having fun at Addy's expense.

Rafe made a choking sound, and Addy frowned at him then shrugged and smiled at Jim. "They're teasing me, Mr.

Castle. No matter how often I try, my fried chicken always ends up burned on the outside or half raw on the inside." She paused, as though for effect. "Sometimes both."

As Rafe and Abby both laughed, admiration for Addy's spunk rose in Jim.

"It's not that bad, sis," Abby said. "And your chocolate cake is the best in the county."

Rafe nodded. "And your catfish is second only to Tuck's."

"Ha. A good thing you said that, Rafe Collins." Abby's smile rested on Rafe, showing affection laced with familiarity.

The lucky cuss. Jim hoped his friend appreciated what he had. He pushed his empty plate aside and leaned back in his chair.

"Don't get too comfortable," Rafe said. "I happen to know there's blackberry cobbler for dessert."

After the meal was finished and Jim and Rafe had been shooed out of the kitchen by Abby, they sat on the front porch.

"I'm really glad to see you back. I've missed our talks." Rafe leaned his hide-bottomed chair back on two legs and stuck a piece of sour dock in his mouth.

Jim chuckled. "Still chewing on that dock I see."

Rafe grinned and shook his head. "Tuck used to try to break me of the habit, but now she says I could be chewing on something a lot worse, like Squeezebox and his tobacco."

"Is the group still together?"

Rafe shook his head. "Mr. Willie passed away last year, and the heart sort of went out of the rest as far as their music goes."

"You mean Abby isn't playing her fiddle anymore? It used to pretty much be the love of her life."

"Oh yes, Tuck still plays for church socials every now and then, and of course we can't have a family get-together without someone begging her for a tune. But Squeezebox Tanner and Tom Black bowed out completely." Rafe winked.

"And I'm the love of her life now."

"Sorry to hear about Squeezebox and Tom."

"It's sad. Tuck tries to get Addy to join her on the piano, but she won't play for anyone but family, and not very often." He flashed a grin. "And speaking of Addy, I think our plan may be working."

Jim shook his head. "I don't know, Rafe. She didn't seem to be that interested in seeing me again."

"That's what you think." Rafe chuckled. "Why do you think she was so nervous? It took a little teasing to get her to loosen up."

The door opened, and Addy stepped out. "Rafe, Abby would like for you to help her get the boys down for a nap if you're not busy."

Rafe cut a glance at Jim then back to his sister-in-law. "Sure I will, if you'll stay out here and talk to Jim. Can't leave company alone, now can we?"

Addy bit her bottom lip. "Of course, I'd be happy to keep Mr. Castle company until you get back."

Jim stood as she stepped out onto the porch. When she eased into a rocking chair, perching on the edge of the seat, he sat back down. "Miss Sullivan. . ."

"I'm so. . ."

They both stopped and laughed.

"Please, Miss Sullivan, you first." He was so happy to see a sparkle in her eye that he could have simply sat in silence and watched her.

"I only wished to apologize for not recognizing you the other day." A pink blush washed over her cheeks. "I knew you looked familiar, but I was rather distracted. When it came to me who you were, I was already at home, so I couldn't very well go back and apologize."

"Of course not." Jim leaned forward. "If anyone should apologize, it's I. I should have identified myself. Instead, I startled you. It's no wonder you bolted." He cringed. That probably wasn't the best word to use.

A smile tipped her lips, causing a tiny dimple to flash. "I did rather bolt, didn't I?"

He couldn't keep from grinning. This wasn't going so badly after all. "So now that we've both apologized, could we put the incident behind us and start over?"

"I would like that very much, Mr. Castle."

"So would I. And if it's not too presumptuous of me, do you think you could bring yourself to call me Jim? After all, we've known each other long enough, it seems."

"That's quite true. We met at Rafe and Abby's wedding. Very well, Jim, and since we're such old friends, you may call me Addy."

Her rippling laughter floated on the air like music, and he absorbed it into his heart and memory. Funny she didn't remember they'd met before the wedding.

three

"Miss Sullivan, did you hear about the train coming in next week?" The gap between Eugene's two front teeth yawned as he flashed a grin at Addy.

"Yes, I did hear that, Gene." She smiled at the little boy standing beside her desk. "That's exciting, isn't it?"

Within seconds the entire class had crowded around her desk, voices raised in excitement and wonder.

Petite Margaret could barely be seen among the taller children, but her voice rang out loud and clear. "I wish I could ride on it. I think I'll ask my mama to let me."

"Aw, you dumb girl. It's a freight train. You can't ride in it."

"Johnny Carroll, shame on you." Addy frowned at the freckled-faced redhead, who was actually one of her favorites. "You apologize to Margaret right this instant."

He mumbled an apology then stood with his hands in his pockets, waiting to see if he'd get more than a reprimand.

"That's better. Please see that there's no more name calling. Now, please take your seats, children." She turned to the blackboard to finish writing the arithmetic problems. When she faced her students again, everyone was seated, anticipation on each face. She smiled. They knew her too well.

"Before we begin our arithmetic, perhaps we'll have a short discussion of current events." As murmurs began, she held up her hand. "In an orderly fashion, please."

A hand popped up from one of the rear seats, followed by several others.

"Yes, Eugene?"

"Pa says the train can't go any farther south 'cause the tracks aren't laid yet."

23

"That's right, Eugene. The White River Line from the north has reached us, but nothing can go farther south until the teams of workers from both directions meet. Then the line will be complete. Yes, Ronald?"

The boy jumped up, eagerness flushing his face. "They're bringing supplies for the town and the railroad."

"Thank you, Ronald." She motioned to Annie Bolton, a tall girl in the front row. "Annie?"

"It's not just supplies. My pa said they're bringing more railroad men to help finish the tracks." She nodded and sat back down.

More railroad workers? Addy frowned. Most of the men were respectful, but some of the newer employees were of a rougher sort. She hated to contemplate the two saloons with more patrons. Occasionally fights spilled out onto the boardwalks. So far, the ones participating in these brawls had been quickly and speedily escorted to the town's improvised jail. But if the town became overrun?

"Well, thank you, Annie." She gave the girl what she hoped was a bright smile. "More citizens for Branson Town. That's very exciting."

"Not as exciting as the train, though," Eugene said.

Johnny Carroll raised his hand.

"All right, Johnny, you're the last one for the day. We need to get on to our regular subjects."

"I was just wonderin', Miss Sullivan. Do you think we could take the day off school to see the train come in?"

Now that wasn't a bad idea. "Perhaps. I'd have to check with the school board. They might agree if we make it a school project."

A groan resounded across the room.

"You mean we'll have to do a report about it?" The woebegone expression on Johnny's face was so comical Addy had to press her lips together to keep from grinning.

"Yes, but perhaps we'll make it a group report. You can all

write down a few things that impress you, and then we'll put them all together." She included the class in her smile.

Annie's hand shot up once more. "Like a story?"

"Exactly, we'll even illustrate it and put it up on the bulletin board for parents' day." As their faces brightened, she hastened to add, "But remember, we have to get permission from the school board first."

One good thing about the formation of the new Branson School District was that it relieved her of certain responsibilities. Such as disappointing her students if the answer was no.

The children were on extra-good behavior the rest of the day, not wanting to risk the possibility of missing the grand, history-making event. Addy didn't blame them. Bolts of excitement charged through her as well.

Of course, to be honest, the near certainty that Jim Castle would be there when the train chugged into the station might have been responsible for a good deal of her eagerness. She frowned and attempted to push the thought away. . . without success.

She'd been surprised at the depth of her attraction toward him that Sunday at her sister's. She'd anticipated seeing him again, believing he felt the same, but nearly three weeks had passed, and she'd seen him only in fleeting moments around town. Usually he tipped his hat and went on his way. Twice he'd paused long enough to exchange civilities.

More than likely she'd only imagined his interest. Embarrassment washed over her. Had her interest in him been obvious? How humiliating if he'd noticed. She'd make sure to be polite but cool the next time she saw him.

That afternoon, when she'd dismissed the class and closed up, she headed for Dr. Gregory Stephens's office. As chairman of the school board, he'd be the one to which she should broach the subject of a field trip to see the train come in.

At the sight of Jim Castle's tall form striding toward her,

she almost turned around and went back to the school, but he'd already spotted her and smiled as he came near. "Addy, how nice to see you." He reached for her hand, and the next thing she knew it was enveloped in his.

Warmth flowed through her fingers, all the way up to her shoulder. She cleared her throat. "Hello, Jim." Oh no, her voice shook. So much for being cool and distant.

Her hand trembled in his. She must get away before he noticed. She spotted the doctor coming out of Brown's Mercantile, an honest excuse to escape. "I'm sorry, I have an appointment. It was nice to see you again as well." Slipping her hand from his, she hurried across the street and approached the doctor.

Well, she would have an appointment if Dr. Stephens wasn't busy. It was only a little fib. Still a pang of guilt shot through her. A lie was a lie.

⁂

Disappointment tugged at Jim as he saw the tall, broad-shouldered doctor take Addy's hand and smile down at her. Were they a courting couple? The expression on the doctor's face sure indicated it.

Of course, it was probably for the best. Jim had known from the beginning there was no chance for him with the lovely Addy. Which was why he'd avoided her since the Sunday dinner at Rafe's house. Rafe must not know about the doctor or surely he'd have mentioned it.

Some other man would be standing by that white picket fence with her, just as he'd thought. Someone who had a stable life right here in Branson Town. Like the doctor. Jim was happy for her. He was. So why the sick feeling inside his gut?

He sauntered down the sidewalk and attempted to focus his thoughts on his upcoming meeting later in the week with Fullbright and the owners of the Maine Exhibition Building. He'd advise them to change the name of the establishment to something that would reflect a local flair. Since it would be constructed on a bluff overlooking the river, he thought Mountain Lodge or White River Lodge would be a good choice. He doubted they'd go for it though. They were pretty stuck on Maine Hunting and Fishing Lodge.

Arriving at the livery stable, he retrieved his horse, Finch, and mounted. A quick ride to Forsyth might help clear his head of Addy and the doctor. He had a couple of telegrams he needed to send anyway. A new park in Virginia had requested his services, but he'd have to let them know it would be at least ten more months before he could leave Branson Town. He'd more than likely lose the job, but there were always more tourism projects to take on.

As he rode down the narrow road, hemmed in by giant oaks and black walnut trees, he whistled a tune. He'd disliked enclosed places since he was a child. The job he'd held at Marvel Cave had helped him overcome that, but he still preferred wide-open spaces.

Relieved, he came out of the woods and into a clearing. He took a deep breath, inhaling the scent of honeysuckle carried by the soft breeze. The fragrance reminded him of Addy, who always smelled like flowers.

He emitted a short laugh. It seemed everything reminded him of Addy lately. And it was hopeless because nothing had changed since he was here before. Even if she cared for him, which she obviously didn't, he'd never ask a woman like her to leave the stability of home and hop from one town to another. His job even took him out of the country at times.

Why couldn't he get the woman out of his mind? She was extremely attractive, but he'd met his share of pretty women, some as pretty as or even prettier than she. So why did he carry her face in his head just about everywhere he went? What was it about her? She wasn't even that nice to him most of the time. And likely she was in love with the doc. A sharp pain stabbed through him.

He urged Finch forward and didn't slow down until he rode into Forsyth. He sent his telegraph messages then wandered down to the docks to watch the steamboats battening down for the night. There were only two docked. Thanks to the railroad, they were a dying breed. The price of progress.

He turned away and went to a local café to grab some supper. The special was corned beef and cabbage, which he despised. Not wanting to take the time to have anything cooked from scratch, he ordered coffee and a ham sandwich.

Someone had left a newspaper on the counter, so he opened it. It was a weekly, and all the news was old, so he busied himself reading the ads. Anything to fill his mind so that thoughts of Addy wouldn't torment him.

By the time Jim got back to Branson Town, everything was shut down except for the hotels and the two saloons. He sat for a moment, tapping his fingers on his leg. He sure didn't need to be alone with his thoughts. Maybe he should ride out to Rafe's and find out what he knew about Addy and the doctor.

After a moment of gnawing at his lip, he thought better of that idea. Abby probably wouldn't take too kindly to his showing up this time of night. Farmers went to bed early.

He rode to the livery stable and saw that his black stallion, Finch, was taken care of and then headed to the hotel on foot.

Cigar smoke hung over a small group of men in the lobby. A heated discussion seemed to be going on. He knew most of them casually. Businessmen or potential businessmen who knew the possibilities of investing in the fledgling town and were willing and able to cash in on it.

One of the men waved a hand. "Castle. Maybe you can clear this debate up for us."

Jim smiled and shook his head. "Another time perhaps. I have a stack of ledgers waiting for my attention." Making his escape, he headed for the stairs only to stop short when he passed the dining room.

Seated at a table across the room, Addy smiled at the doctor, who leaned forward, his eyes intent on hers.

Jim's face tightened, and his body tensed. So that was that. Apparently they were courting. With a heavy heart, he turned away and headed up the stairs to his suite.

four

Two straight lines of eager students filed out of the classroom and lined up behind Mrs. Carroll and Mrs. Bright, who had volunteered to help with the field trip.

Addy and fourteen-year-old Annie Brown made up the rear guard to make sure no overly adventurous children decided to head out on their own.

Annie darted a nervous glance at the girls, standing tallest to shortest in her line. "Miss Sullivan," she whispered, "the boys' line isn't in order." She motioned toward the front.

Sure enough, a curly mop of red hair poked out from behind Thomas Carter, a tall thirteen-year-old at the head of the line.

Addy pressed her lips together to hold back a smile. Johnny. She walked up the line and stopped beside him then tapped her foot as she looked down at the culprit.

Johnny glanced up, and his eyes widened. "Oops. Guess I must have lost my bearings, teacher."

"Yes, I believe you did," Addy said. "Shall I hold your hand and lead you to your place?"

Thomas guffawed, and Johnny's face flamed. "No, ma'am. I reckon I can find it all right."

Addy shot a look of reprimand at Thomas then motioned for Johnny to precede her to the end of the line, where he scooted in between Harry and Eugene. She patted him on the shoulder then blew a small whistle to get everyone's attention. "Children, we have a place reserved for us at the depot where everyone should be able to see just fine. So please stay in your places. Otherwise we won't be able to keep track of everyone."

Johnny ducked his head then looked up at her. "Sorry, Miss Sullivan."

"It's all right, Johnny. I'm sure you won't do it again."

Addy couldn't help a surge of pride as the two lines filed across the schoolyard then down the boardwalk, the boys marching like soldiers, the girls with perfect deportment. She only hoped it would last.

A crowd thronged the road by the depot.

Addy covered her nose and mouth with her plain white handkerchief to keep the flying dust from her throat.

Several of the children began to cough.

"Children, cover your mouths until we get to the station." Someone bumped into her, and bodies rushed by, obscuring her view. Panic rose as she searched ahead for the children.

"Make way, there. Can't you see there are women and young children trying to get through?" Dr. Stephens's booming voice sounded angelic to Addy at the moment.

With mixed feelings of relief and dread, she allowed him to take her arm and guide her and the rest of the group across the road and onto the depot's wooden platform.

"Now, boys and girls, stand still and don't move until your teacher says the word," the doctor said.

She smiled and held out her hand. "Thank you, doctor. Now I really must count heads and make sure we're all here before we go to find our place."

"I'd be more than happy to assist you. In fact, I thought you might need my help with the children today."

"Oh, that's kind of you, but. . ." Addy tried to protest, but his hand grasped her elbow, and before she knew it she, the children, and the two mothers had been herded to the spot designated for them.

She managed to retrieve her elbow and turned to check on her young charges. "Move back a little more, children. You're too near the edge of the platform. Mrs. Bright, if you can stay there at the end, and Mrs. Carroll, will you please stand at the center of this row?"

She soon had them all settled, the older children behind the younger ones with the adults and older children dispersed evenly among them.

A shadow of disappointment crossed the doctor's face as he saw they were separated by an entire row of children. She silently congratulated herself.

The week before when she'd accepted his dinner invitation, she'd regretted it almost immediately. What she'd thought was merely a dinner meeting to discuss the field trip had turned out to be an evening of revelation by the doctor of his need for a wife and hints that she was his number-one choice for the position. She'd managed to avoid him since then. Until now.

A roar of excited voices surrounded her, and the crowd surged forward. She stepped in closer to her students and glanced down the rows, then on down the platform.

Through an opening in the throng, she spotted Jim. Their eyes locked. An electric charge ran through her, and she stared, helpless to look away.

The sound of the train's steam whistle broke the spell, and she whirled around. The engine wasn't in sight yet, but the chugging sound as it slowed could be heard clearly, and once more the shrill whistle rent the air.

A collective sigh made its way through the crowd. Then the engine came around the bend, and a roar exploded from the enthusiastic men, women, and children. Hats flew into the air.

Addy couldn't make a sound. Excitement and un-explainable joy surged through her. Her eyes took in first the engine and then the boxcars that followed.

She'd seen trains before, even ridden on one once when her family had taken a trip to Kansas City. But to actually see it, shining and black, smoke pouring forth, right here in Branson Town was enough to render her speechless. A whole new world was opening. As soon as the southern tracks were completed, the passenger trains would run.

Addy's breathing quickened, and in her mind's eye she saw herself climbing aboard and rolling away from the station. Away from Branson Town. Maybe even away from Missouri.

Would she dare? But how could she? Leave Pa and Ma and Abby? Whatever had gotten into her?

The engine slowed to a crawl, and its loud squeal seemed to go on forever as it came to a stop in front of the depot.

The roar of the crowd finally faded to a murmur as a man in a dark-blue suit stepped down and onto the platform.

Mr. Fullbright stepped forward and extended his hand. "I'd like to welcome the White River Line to Branson Town, Missouri."

❧

Jim's gaze drifted from the welcoming speech and down the platform to rest upon Addy. Her face glowed with excitement, and even from several yards away, he could see the sparkle in her eyes. A grin split his face. He'd never seen her this animated.

Instead of following Fullbright and the newly arrived White River Line representative across to the waiting carriage, he began to push his way through the crowd toward Addy.

Spotting the doctor in the midst of the children, he hesitated, and then taking a deep breath, he stepped resolutely forward once more. He had to at least speak to her and share her excitement for a moment.

"Jim!" He turned to see Fullbright motioning to him from the street, an expression of impatience on his usually placid face.

He turned to look at Addy once more, but the crowd was so thick he could no longer see her.

Stalking across the platform, he stepped onto the street and climbed into the carriage after Fullbright.

❧

Addy scanned the area where only a moment before Jim had

appeared to be coming toward her. Now he was nowhere to be seen.

Disappointed, she motioned to her assistants. Time to go back to the classroom for another two hours.

"Miss Sullivan, I'd be happy to escort you and the children back to the school." Dr. Stephens had once more appeared at her side.

"Thank you, doctor, but that really isn't necessary." She smiled and motioned to Annie and the ladies. "As you can see, I have plenty of helpers."

"Oh, well, if you're certain." He hesitated. "I wonder if you've thought any more about the matter we discussed at dinner last week."

"Well, no. I'm afraid I haven't. I've been dreadfully busy." If only he would drop the subject. Addy didn't want to hurt the man's feelings. He was very kind and quite good looking, if one liked the large, ruddy type. Addy wished she were interested in him. He'd probably be a fine husband. Unfortunately, she wasn't the slightest bit attracted to him, and he rather bored her.

"Then perhaps you'd care to join me on a picnic this weekend, and we could discuss the subject more thoroughly."

Panicking, she grasped around in her mind for a reasonable excuse to refuse. Taking her silence for acceptance, he smiled. "I'll be at your home Saturday morning at eleven then. Please don't worry about the food. I'll have my landlady pack us a lunch."

Addy watched in helpless consternation as he walked away.

A laugh drew her attention. Johnny's mother looked at her with kind amusement on her face. "Apparently, the good doctor is smitten enough he can't tell when he's refused."

A short laugh escaped Addy's throat. "Is it that obvious?"

"Well, it was to me. Apparently not to him, though." Mrs. Carroll grinned and turned aside to help get the children lined up.

The trek to the school was uneventful. After Mrs. Bright

and Mrs. Carroll said good-bye, Addy turned to the excited class and held up her hand to quiet them. "I thought this important event called for a celebration, so I brought cookies from home this morning."

Cheers rang out, and once more Addy held up her hand. "Before we have our party, I have a short assignment for you, so please take out your tablets and pencils."

She waited until the rustle stopped before continuing. "I'd like for you to write down as many things about today's event as you can think of in the next ten minutes. Afterward we shall have our cookies."

"Do we turn our papers in, teacher?" Eugene asked.

"Not today. You can finish them over the weekend and bring them with you on Monday. Then we'll see how much combined information we have for our group report."

While the class concentrated on their assignment, Addy's thoughts drifted back over the afternoon. She couldn't think of a time she'd been this excited. At least, not since Papa Jack took her and Abby on his riverboat, the *Julia Dawn*.

She'd never shared with anyone how much she'd loved that experience. Drops of moisture from the river spraying across her skin. The smell of lumber and other supplies Pa had transported up and down the river. The train's whistle had reminded her of the escaping steam from the *Julia Dawn*'s smokestack.

She sighed. It had broken her heart when Pa sold the boat, and she could tell it was hard for him, too. But he'd needed the money that first year of farming, and if he'd kept the boat, maybe he and Ma couldn't have married and adopted her and Abby.

Would she ever find a love like Pa and Ma's? She sighed again. Probably not.

Jim's cool demeanor and warm eyes filled her thoughts. She'd truly thought he returned her admiration, but she must have been wrong. She knew so little about men. What a silly goose she was. She'd even believed he was coming over to speak to her at the depot this afternoon. Then the next moment he'd totally disappeared.

She simply had to stop thinking about him. He'd be leaving in a few months anyway. Maybe it would be easier to get him out of her mind once he was gone.

"Miss Sullivan?" The stage whisper from the front row snapped her out of her reverie.

"Yes, Margaret?" She shook her head to dispel unwanted thoughts.

"We've been writing an awful long time."

Addy lifted the chain and looked at her watch. She smiled. It had been twelve minutes. "Mercy, you're right, Margaret."

The day ended on a high note for the children, with the cookies being a success and their excitement about the coming weekend.

For Addy, however, the day, which had begun with such high expectations, now seemed dismal. She simply had to make herself snap out of it. Perhaps a picnic with the doctor wasn't such a bad idea after all. Why should she let Jim Castle affect her emotions like this?

five

Addy shivered as a thrill of excitement ran through her, and she stared as Pa slapped a huge spoon of mashed potatoes onto his plate then passed the bowl to Ma.

"Pa, are you sure? The State of Maine's exhibition building? The big log building we saw at the World's Fair?" After the gloom of her afternoon, she welcomed this bit of good news. Even if it seemed impossible.

"That's right, daughter." Pa nodded as he spooned green beans from the rose-printed serving bowl. "Jim Castle told Rafe they've already disassembled it in St. Louis."

"And it's for sure going to be a hunting lodge? Right here in Branson?"

He nodded and passed the vegetable bowl to Ma. "They're bringing the sections by train, and when it's reassembled we'll have a hunting lodge overlooking the White River."

How exciting. They would probably hire local folks to cook and wait tables and clean. Maybe she could get a job there.

A shock jolted her. What in the world was wrong with her? She couldn't give up her teaching position to work at a hunting lodge. The very idea.

"I thought Abby, Rafe, and the boys were coming for supper tonight." She'd actually been looking forward to a nice long talk with her sister.

Ma placed a small piece of roast on Betty's plate and began cutting it up. "Change of plans. We're having a picnic tomorrow. If you don't have school work tonight, maybe you could help me cook?"

"As long as you don't make me fry chicken." Addy made a

face at Pa, who chuckled.

Ma cast a slight frown at her. "Now Addy, you just need more practice and you'll do fine. Perhaps you should fry the chicken, after all."

A choking sound from Pa drew their attention. He shook his head.

"Fine, Pa. It had crossed my mind to make your favorite pineapple upside-down cake." She smiled. "Maybe I will anyway."

It would be nice to spend the day with the whole family and would give her a chance for that talk with Abby. They hadn't had an outing by the river in quite a while.

Suddenly she gasped. Oh no. She'd promised to go on a picnic with the doctor. She bit her lip. "Ma, would it be all right if Dr. Stephens joined us?"

Surprise filled Ma's eyes, and creases appeared between her brows, but she quickly smiled. "Of course."

Addy frowned. She knew that look. "Now Ma, don't get any ideas. He invited me to go on a picnic with him, and before I could think up an excuse, he presumed the answer was yes."

"Why, I had no ideas at all. You have a perfect right to have friends. Even gentlemen friends."

Pa cleared his throat. "Do I have a right to an opinion?"

Addy stared at her pa, half hoping he'd forbid her to see the doctor.

"Dr. Stephens is a fine man. You could do worse."

"Trying to marry me off, Pa?" Addy was only half joking. After all, she wasn't getting any younger. Maybe her parents were tired of having her around. The familiar pang of loneliness ran through her, and she caught her breath.

"Nope. I'd keep all my daughters single at home forever if it was up to me." Pa shook his head. "Of course Abby had other ideas, and I'm sure you will, too, someday."

Betty's sweet voice rang out. "I'll never get married

and leave you, Pa."

"That's my girl." Pa lifted her onto his lap and kissed her cheek.

Addy smiled. She had to stop imagining things. Pa and Ma loved her, and she'd be welcome here as long as she wanted to stay. "Maybe I'll stay home, too. You and I can be old maids together, Betty girl."

A little frown crossed Betty's face. "I thought I'd be a teacher like you. I don't want to be a maid."

Addy laughed. "Me either." Unless she could be one at the new lodge. Oh. There she went again. She must get these ideas out of her head.

After the table was cleared and the dishes washed and put away, Addy joined her family on the wide front porch. She leaned back in her chair and shut her eyes for a moment. She loved the sound of night birds and didn't even mind the chirping of insects.

Mosquitoes buzzed and flitted. Her eyes shot open, and she slapped one away from her ear. Mosquitoes she could do without.

"Is Aunt Kate coming to the picnic? I noticed she wasn't at church last Sunday." Addy loved Ma's Aunt Kate. In spite of her strict ideas, she was gentle and loving. Always had been with Addy and Abby.

"I don't think so, dear." Worry shadowed Ma's eyes. "She's not feeling well lately. You and Abby really need to visit her more often. She misses you."

Guilt pricked her. "I'm sorry. I'll stop by Uncle Will's after school on Monday."

"That would be nice." Ma leaned back on the swing, resting her head against Pa's shoulder.

Addy gave them a wistful glance. Even after all these years, they were still sweethearts. Jim's face flashed across her mind, and exasperated, she jumped up. "I think I'll go inside and work on an assignment for Monday since we'll be busy tomorrow."

Betty clapped her hands, and her eyes danced. "I can't wait for the picnic tomorrow."

Ma smiled at her youngest. "It'll be so much fun, won't it?"

Addy bid good night to all. She usually looked forward to family get-togethers, but knowing the doctor would be there spoiled it for her. Why hadn't she simply made an excuse and told him no?

꙳

Addy couldn't help being amused at the look of disappointment that crossed the doctor's countenance. For a moment she'd thought he would protest the new arrangement.

"But. . .but. . .I'd hoped. . ." Slowly resignation crossed his face, and his shoulders drooped. "Of course, if your family is also having a picnic, we'll join them. Yes, that's only right."

"Thank you for understanding, doctor." She smiled as he took the basket full of food from her then helped her into the buggy.

As they led the way to the picnic site near the river, he turned to her and smiled. "We'll have a nice day in spite of. . . That is, we'll have a nice day I'm sure with your family."

"Yes, doctor, we will."

He cleared his throat. "Miss Sullivan, I was wondering if you would mind calling me Gregory."

Panic gripped Addy, and her chest tightened. How to get out of this one? If she agreed to call him by his Christian name, he'd be sure to take it as a sign that she wanted him to court her. Which she most certainly did not.

"Well, Dr. Stephens, don't you think that would be a little premature? After all, we haven't known each other very long."

"No, no, of course you're right," he said. "Please forgive me for making the suggestion."

"That's quite all right. No offense taken, I assure you." Addy breathed a sigh of relief to have gotten out of it so easily. "Look, there's the picnic spot."

The doctor turned the horses into the clearing and stopped beneath a towering oak tree. Abby and Rafe's wagon was already there, and Rafe had thrown together some boards for makeshift tables.

David and Dawson sat on a quilt in the sunshine, tumbling over each other in an attempt to reach the tall blades of grass.

Abby threw her hands up in the air. "Yay! You're here. Betty, will you please watch your nephews and keep them from getting too far from the quilt?"

Betty giggled, and a smile creased her face. "Sure, Aunt Tuck." She ran for the boys, who let out screams of rapture when they saw her.

Ma shook her head. "Abby, I wish you would discourage her calling you Aunt Tuck."

"Aw, Ma. She hears Rafe call me Tuck, and I don't mind. I think it's kind of cute."

Addy laughed and nodded at the three children tumbling about on the blanket. "I think we've got a three-member mutual admiration society."

"I know. Isn't it adorable?" Abby nodded at the doctor. "I'm glad you could join us, Dr. Stephens." But the look she threw Addy warned that a question-and-answer session between them was coming up soon.

The chance came a few minutes later, when the doctor reluctantly followed Pa and Rafe to the river to fish.

While Ma was occupied taking food out of one of the baskets, Abby sidled up to Addy as she set out silver on another table. "Okay, what's going on with the doc, sister dear?"

Addy shook her head. "Not a thing on my part. I think he's got his heart set on marrying me."

Abby laughed. "Well, don't you think bringing him to a picnic might encourage that idea just a little bit?"

"Well, I guess. I think I got snookered into it. One minute he was asking, and the next he was telling me when he'd pick me up." Addy frowned. "I didn't know how to get out of it."

Abby snorted. "You always were too nice."

"Yes, well, don't forget your own experience with a certain doctor."

"Eww, you're right. Sometimes we get ourselves in a pickle jar with no way to reach the top."

"Well, this is one pickle that's floating to the top. I'm going to tell him later that I'm not a bit interested." Addy gave an emphatic nod.

"Too bad he's here. Jim Castle will be here any second. And I don't think he's coming to spend time with Rafe and me."

Addy couldn't stop the gasp from escaping. "Oh, Abby. Did you invite him?"

"He sort of invited himself. I think he's falling hard for you, sis."

Addy's heart raced. "You're imagining things, Abby. Stop teasing."

"Okay, suit yourself." At the sound of wheels and horses' hooves, Abby grinned. "Here he is now."

Sure enough, Jim's buggy pulled into the clearing. He jumped down and threw his reins over a branch. He doffed his hat and flashed that devastating, mind-numbing smile of his. "Good afternoon, ladies. I hope I haven't missed the picnic."

Abby laughed, and glee shone all over her face. "Not at all, Jim. We're just now setting things out. The men are fishing if you'd like to join them."

"Maybe later." He turned to Addy, and his eyes seemed to blaze into hers. "I'm sorry I missed you at the depot yesterday. I was unavoidably detained for a moment, and then you had disappeared."

"Oh, did you wish to speak with me about something, Mr. Castle?"

"I thought we'd dispensed with formalities, Addy."

Heat washed over her face. Oh dear. He was right. That

had probably been a mistake made in a moment of romantic foolishness. Anyway, what would the doctor think if she called Jim by his given name after refusing to do the same for him? Oh, so what? She didn't care what the doctor thought. Jim had been a friend of Rafe's for a long time, and that made the difference.

"Yes, I believe we did. Jim, then." She smiled.

"Oh, look who's coming." Abby chortled. "Why I do believe it's your date, Addy."

⋆

Jim scowled as the doctor came into sight, followed by Rafe and Jack Sullivan.

The doctor's glance went to Jim then to Addy.

Jim watched in surprise as Dr. Stephens stepped over to Addy and put his hand on her arm. That was overly familiar unless there was an understanding between them.

"Is there anything I can do to help?" Dr. Stephens asked.

Addy frowned and moved away from the doctor's hand. "No, I think we have everything under control."

Jim glanced from Addy to the doctor and narrowed his eyes. Was she interested in the man or not? If so, he'd bow out. But the look in her eyes when she'd spotted Jim yesterday and then again today told him she had feelings not for the doctor but for him. And he wasn't giving up until he knew for sure.

Suddenly she stepped over to him. "Jim, have you met Dr. Stephens? Doctor, this is Jim Castle."

The doctor looked as though he might choke.

Jim almost laughed. Had Addy made a statement by calling him Jim? Maybe he was making too much of that, but it was something to grab ahold of anyway.

Mrs. Sullivan cast a startled glance at Addy and both men. She stepped over to her husband and laid her hand on his. "Everything is ready, Jack. Will you ask the blessing, please?"

They bowed their heads.

"Dear gracious heavenly Father," Jack said, "we thank You for this food You've supplied from Your bounty. Please bless it, bless those who prepared it and all who've come together to partake of it."

As Jack continued praying, Jim sent up a special request of his own. *God, this woman is mine. Please see that she knows that.*

Hmm. Maybe that prayer wasn't exactly reverent. He'd have to talk to the Lord about it later.

six

Dr. Stephens stood with his plate and Addy's in hand and nodded toward a spot beneath an apple tree, some distance from the rest of their group. "That apple tree is a nice place for us."

Addy frowned. "Oh, but don't you think that would be rather impolite? I think I'd prefer to sit near my family."

A grimace passed over the doctor's face. "Really, Adeline. How will we ever plan our future if we're never alone?"

Addy's jaw dropped, and she snapped it firmly shut. Her nostrils flared, and her throat constricted while drawing in a deep breath. This had gone on long enough. "Dr. Stephens, I don't know where you got the idea you and I have a future. I'm sure I haven't encouraged that thought in any way."

He gave her an astonished look. "But I told you that you were my choice for a wife."

She planted her hands on her hips and glared at him. "Yes, you did hint at that possibility, but did I at any time indicate I was interested in marrying you?"

He closed his eyes for a moment and took a deep breath, letting it seep out while throwing her a look he'd give a child. "I can see I've been too hasty, rushing you like this. Please forgive me. I'll take things more slowly."

"You will not take things any way at all concerning me. I'm more than happy to be your friend, but I can assure you that is all we shall ever be."

His face flamed red. "Then perhaps I'd better leave." He placed both dishes on the table.

"Nonsense. You are quite welcome to stay and enjoy the picnic with us." Not exactly true, but it would be the height

45

of rudeness to tell him what she really thought.

"I don't think so. Of course, I will be happy to drive you home if you wish to leave now." He gave her a look that was almost comical in its hopefulness.

"No, I don't wish to leave. I'm very sorry for the misunderstanding, doctor. I hope we can remain friends."

He gave a short nod and stalked off to his buggy.

The tightness in Addy's neck and jaw eased as the doctor departed. But a surge of guilt mixed in with the relief as he drove away. She could have avoided the incident if she'd had the wisdom and courage to tell him how she felt from the beginning.

"The good doctor had to leave?" She spun around at the sound of Jim's voice.

"Yes, I suppose he did."

He raised his eyebrow, but she didn't speak, so he turned to the table and glanced at the two filled plates. "I assume one of these is yours."

She smiled and picked up the doctor's plate, raking the food back into the serving dishes. She then picked up her own plate and smiled at Jim. "Let's join the family. We're missing all the fun."

Jim placed his hand beneath her elbow, but she gently moved her arm. She wasn't giving him ideas either. As much as she liked him and enjoyed his company, there were obstacles to any type of relationship between them other than friendship. The main one being that his job would take him away before long.

"You two slowpokes hurry, or we'll eat without you." Rafe winked. "Don't worry, Jim. Addy didn't fry the chicken."

"Be careful"—Addy threw a mock frown at her brother-in-law—"or I might not let you have any of my chocolate cake that you like so much."

The meal and banter went on for nearly an hour before the men headed back to the river to fish while the women put the children down for naps. With that accomplished, they sat on the ground beneath a wide spreading oak.

"What was that with the doctor, Adeline?" Ma waved a mosquito away from Betty then glanced at her daughter.

"What do you mean, Ma?" Addy blushed. She knew very well what her mother spoke of.

"He left rather suddenly. Did he have medical duties to attend?"

"No, I don't think so." Addy bit her lip. She may as well tell Ma the truth. "He somehow imagined that I was willing to enter into a long-term relationship with him."

"He wanted to marry you?" No beating around the bush with Ma.

"Yes, ma'am. When I told him we could only be friends, he decided to leave."

"I see." Ma nodded, and Addy held her breath waiting for what her mother would have to say next. "Well dear, I don't think he quite suited you. I hope you told him kindly."

"Well, perhaps I might have been a little more gentle." At the thought of the doctor's presumption, her teeth clenched. "But he made me so mad. He rather took things for granted."

"Besides, she has a hankering for someone else." Abby laughed and slapped her overalled knee. Addy's twin took any chance that came along to wear her favorite clothing.

"Behave yourself, Abby. I do not."

"Oh no? I think you do. I think you're falling hard for Jim. But that's okay. He's already fallen for you." Her blue eyes sparkled.

Addy blushed. "I guess I am rather falling for him, as you say. But it can't go anywhere."

"Why not? Jim's a great fellow." Abby frowned.

"Do you want me to move away?" Addy gave her sister an intent look.

Abby gasped. "No, of course not. Oh sister, I hadn't thought ahead that far. Well, Jim will just have to stay in

Branson. Plenty of jobs. Mr. Fullbright will have to find something for him to do around here."

A glimmer of hope shimmered inside Addy. Would Jim even consider staying in Branson? With all the new businesses and the tourism, there should be work for him here, shouldn't there? But why should he? He wasn't that interested in her. A bee buzzed by her face, and she swatted it away then laughed. "Don't be silly, Abby. And stop imagining things. Jim Castle and I are only friends.

❧

Jim couldn't believe his luck. He'd offered to take Addy home, fully expecting a resounding no after the lambasting she'd given the doctor.

Instead, she'd lowered those beautiful blue eyes for a moment then lifted them and murmured a soft, "Thank you. That's very kind of you."

Now as the horse trotted down the road toward the Sullivan farm, the sway of the buggy created a lazy rocking-chair effect. Jim glanced toward Addy on the seat next to him. Her eyelashes rested on her cheek, and a half smile tilted one corner of her mouth.

"Oh!" She sat up, a startled expression on her face. "I almost fell asleep. Please excuse my lack of manners."

Jim grinned. "Not at all. I came close to nodding off myself."

She smiled. "It's been a lovely day."

"It has. Too bad it has to end." Perhaps he could stretch it out a little longer.

She slipped her hand into her pocket and retrieved a lacy handkerchief. Fanning it in front of her face, she said, "I hope it cools off a little soon. Rain would be nice."

Okay, small talk was fine, but they'd be at her home in a few minutes, and he'd like to talk about something besides the weather. "Did your class enjoy their outing to see the train come in?" There, that was better than the weather.

Animation brightened her face. "Oh yes. They were so excited. We're doing a class project on the historical event with pictures and stories. We may also have a play of sorts. It will be a nice end-of-school program for the parents, don't you think?"

"I should think so, yes," he said.

"I can hardly believe the change in Branson Town. The new hotels and other buildings make it seem like a completely different place." Suddenly she turned toward him, her eyes bright with excitement. "Speaking of historical events, would you mind telling me about the new hunting lodge?"

Surprised, he stared at her for a moment. Now why would a lovely young woman be interested in a hunting lodge? "I'd be happy to tell you anything you'd like to know. Within the limits of my knowledge of it, of course."

"Is it true that the State of Maine is being reassembled here?" Her eyes were wide and her lips slightly open.

Jim resisted the impulse to catch his breath. Her beauty was almost too much to bear. He wanted nothing more at the moment than to lean over and kiss those luscious lips. If she only knew how inviting they were, he was certain she'd be horrified.

Pulling himself together, he licked his own lips. If she knew what he was thinking, she'd slap the tar out of him and send him packing. "Er. . .yes, yes, the State of Maine Exhibition has been disassembled and is on its way here. Are you interested in the building?"

"Oh yes. Pa took us to the World's Fair in St. Louis. The State of Maine exhibition was my favorite. The World's Fair was the most exciting thing. Actually, the only exciting thing that I've ever done, except for when Pa took Abby and me with him on the *Julia Dawn*."

Delight ran through Jim from his head to his toes just watching her excitement. "The *Julia Dawn*?"

She laughed. "That was Pa's steamboat. He used to

haul cargo up and down the White River and even the Mississippi."

"I had no idea. I thought your father had always been a farmer." Yet he could imagine Jack Sullivan as a riverboat captain. There was something in the man's demeanor, as though he was comfortable issuing orders.

"Yes, when Addy and I were eight years old our real father died. Our ma had died years before, so we had no one. Papa Jack gave up his business and married Ma Lexie. Then they adopted us."

Jack pulled up alongside her front porch just as the sun sank below the horizon. "It sounds as though they must have loved you very much."

"Yes, they do. And I love them." Suddenly she stopped talking and furrowed her brow at him. "Why, we're here already. Oh dear, I've been talking nonstop. And such frivolous talk at that. Please do forgive me." Before Jim had a chance to say a word or to get down to help her from the buggy, she murmured a hasty thank you, jumped down, and hurried into the house.

He sat there for a while, his heart pounding. So, sweet Addy Sullivan had an adventurous streak. Who would have guessed it? He turned his buggy and headed back to town, barely able to keep his feet from tapping a reel on the buggy's floor.

❧

Stupid, stupid, stupid. How could she have gone on like that? She must have sounded like a school girl.

Addy yanked off the ribbon that held back her curls and tossed it on the washstand. She dipped her hand in the washbasin's cold water and splashed it on her heated face. After dabbing it with a dry towel, she dropped into the rocking chair by the window and closed her eyes.

What exactly had she said to Jim? She forced herself to go over every word of their mostly one-sided conversation.

As far as she could remember, she'd never bared her soul to anyone the way she had to Jim Castle in those few short minutes. If they hadn't arrived home when they did, she would have gone on to tell him about her secret dreams of traveling the world. Things she'd never revealed to anyone. Even Abby. What must he think of her?

She groaned. At best he'd think her a foolish, childish woman. At worst? Her face flamed. At worst he'd think she was in love with him and trying to impress him. He must be terribly amused. Probably laughing his head off.

She sat up straight and took a deep breath. Well, she'd simply have to correct that misassumption. But how? Avoid him? Probably not possible. Well, then failing that, she would ignore him except, of course, for common courtesy. He might wonder why she'd suddenly changed, but better that than the other. Better that than for him to feel sorry for her for making a big fool of herself.

seven

The whistle announced the train's arrival just as school let out.

Addy smiled and shook her head as several of the older boys took off in the direction of the depot. A flash of red tried to get past her, but she grabbed the collar of Johnny's plaid shirt before he could accomplish his mission.

"Hey!" He broke off his yell as he saw who held him captive. "Aw, Miss Sullivan. Can't I go?"

Addy turned loose of the shirt and smoothed it. "Your mother will be expecting you at home, Johnny. You wouldn't want her to worry, would you?"

Resignation crossed his face, and a loud sigh *whoosh*ed from his throat. "No, ma'am."

"That's a good boy. Now run along home." She smiled as he tromped slowly across the schoolyard and down the street. Then she glanced around. Now where was her horse and buggy? She bit her lip. It wasn't like Bobby to be late. She tapped her booted foot and looked up and down the street. No sign of the boy.

With a sigh, she started across the schoolyard in the direction of the livery stable. Several men and boys ran past, stirring up dust. Addy covered her mouth and nose, resisting a sneeze.

Mrs. Clancy, who cooked lunch at one of the cafés, trudged past.

"Where's everyone going?" Addy asked.

"Depot I reckon." Mrs. Clancy didn't bother to stop.

"What's going on?" Addy called after her.

She shrugged and walked on.

Probably just checking out the train. Addy supposed it would be a novelty for some time. She couldn't imagine the uproar once the passenger cars began running.

Laughter and shouts reached her ears, and she hesitated and glanced toward the depot where a crowd was forming. She turned toward the livery then stopped, glancing back to the depot. She really should get her buggy and go. She'd promised to visit her great-aunt Kate today. Still, it wouldn't hurt to just find out what all the excitement was about. If it was anything Uncle Will needed to know, she could pass the information on to him. Yes, she'd better check it out.

The depot wasn't as crowded as it had been when the first train had pulled into the station, but excitement buzzed through the small crowd. One of the cars had been unhitched and stood by the loading dock while a second was unhooked.

Addy shaded her eyes with one hand and peered across, trying to see what the cars contained.

"What do you think it is?"

Addy glanced around and saw a woman tugging on her husband's arm.

"Could be all the parts and supplies for the hunting lodge," the man said.

"Huh!" his wife said. "Well, don't you go getting any ideas about that."

He laughed. "Like I could afford to go there anyway."

The engine began to chug slowly down the track, leaving the two cars behind.

A group of men headed for the loading dock. The doors on the side of the car slid open with a screech.

Addy held her hands over her ears until the doors were completely open. Curiosity overtaking her, she walked down the platform toward the car.

"Addy!" She'd know that voice anywhere. Whirling around, she spied Jim rushing toward her.

She couldn't prevent the rapid thumping of her heart at the sight of him. She clenched her fists at her side and composed herself. She must be polite but aloof. "Yes?"

"It could be dangerous once they start unloading. You need to move to the other end of the platform."

She stared at him. How dare he tell her what she needed to do? "I'm not a child, Mr. Castle. I believe I can take care of myself, thank you."

He took a step backward, his eyes dark with confusion. "I'm sure you can. I simply don't want you to get hurt. Will you please step back out of harm's way?"

"Castle! Get that woman out of the way and make sure no one else gets too close."

Addy's face flamed at the burly man's commands. She should have moved when Jim asked her to. "Excuse me, Mr. Castle." She slipped past him and hurried away.

"Addy!"

Her heart jumped at the sound of his voice, but she hurried down the steps and onto the street.

⛄

Jim scratched his head and watched Addy stomp off. What had he done to rile her up? He'd been so pleased at the way things went at the picnic. Why was she angry? Well, he didn't have time to go after her, even if that would do any good. Women.

"Castle, I need you to help me check these items off."

Jim lifted his hand in acknowledgment and went to assist the new owners of the State of Maine Exhibition Building.

⛄

"Miss Sullivan." Bobby pulled the buggy up alongside her and stopped.

"Bobby, where in the world have you been?" Her voice sounded harsh even to her own ears.

"Looking for you, ma'am." He jumped down. "I had to run an errand for Mr. Jacobs before I could bring your rig to you.

Then when I got to the school, you weren't there. Sorry I was late."

"All right, Bobby. It wasn't your fault. I'm sorry I snapped at you." She climbed into the buggy and took the reins. "Get in and I'll take you back to the stable."

"That's okay. I'm going to find out what's going on at the depot. Do you know what the train brought in?"

Addy bit her lip. She supposed it was the supplies for the lodge but wasn't sure. If only she hadn't gotten so flustered she'd still be there watching them unload. Oh well, why should she care anyway? "No, I don't. Sorry."

She was halfway home before she remembered she was supposed to go to her great-aunt Kate's house. Turning the horse, she headed cross-country to the road that led to the Rayton farm. She had to pull herself together before she got there. Aunt Kate didn't miss anything.

A sigh escaped her lips. What was wrong with her lately? She'd always been the calm, levelheaded twin. Now she was as flighty as Abby used to be. Worse even. Of course, she'd always had that secret desire for adventure, but she'd managed to keep it under control. In two days she'd been incredibly rude to two men. And she was pretty sure she was in love with one of them. What if someone besides family had witnessed her berating the doctor? Even if he was presuming and controlling. And what would people think of her if she did something foolish? Such as quit her job and work for a hunting lodge? Or jump on a train and travel across America?

She pulled to a stop alongside Aunt Kate's porch and sat unmoving. She took several deep breaths in an attempt to control her rambling thoughts. Aunt Kate deserved her full attention.

The door flew open, and Uncle Will's wife, Aunt Sarah, stepped onto the porch. "Land's sake, Addy. What are you sitting out here for? Come on inside."

Ma's younger brother, Will, married Sarah Jenkins the same year Ma and Pa got married. At first Addy had felt a little bit strange calling her Aunt Sarah. She was only nine or ten years older than Addy and Abby. But Ma would have whipped her good if she'd ever called an adult by her first name only.

"Is Aunt Kate at home?" Addy climbed down from the buggy and walked up the steps of the weathered old log cabin. Uncle Will really needed to paint or whitewash the place.

"Of course. She seldom goes anywhere these days except church." She darted a glance at the door then turned to Addy. "I'm a little worried about her. I know she's getting older, but it's like her energy just drained out of her all of a sudden."

"Maybe she should see the doctor." In spite of Addy's anger towards Dr. Stephens, she had confidence in his medical knowledge.

"She refuses to go. I'd hoped Lexie could talk some sense into her. Or one of you girls. She never takes me seriously." The worry lines in her face showed her concern.

Addy nodded. "I'll talk to her, but Ma's the one who can influence her better than anyone."

Aunt Kate sat on the settee in the parlor, a box of mending beside her. Her eyes brightened when they rested on Addy. She laid down the shirt she was mending and started to stand. "Addy." Her voice sounded weak.

"Please don't stand up, Auntie." Addy rushed over to her and, bending down, planted a kiss on her cheek.

Aunt Kate grabbed her hand and squeezed it. "I'm so glad you came. Sit across from me there so I can see you while we talk."

Addy obediently sat on the little rocking chair. As she got a better look at her aunt, she had to force herself not to react. In the three weeks since she'd seen her, something had taken its toll on Aunt Kate.

"Auntie, I hear you haven't been feeling well lately." *Lord, please help me convince her she needs to see a doctor.*

"Oh, everyone fusses over me too much." She shot a fiery look at Sarah. "It's only indigestion. I'm fine."

"Hmmm." Addy nodded. "You're probably right, Auntie. But you know there has been a lot of sickness going around."

Aunt Kate pressed her lips together and frowned. "I said I'm fine."

"I know, I know. I was just thinking of Sam and Larry."

At the mention of Will and Sarah's boys, Aunt Kate's head shot up. "What about Sam and Larry?"

"Well, nothing." Addy smiled at her aunt. "Except I know you wouldn't want to take a chance on passing something along to them. I mean, just in case you have something contagious."

Aunt Kate pierced Addy with her glare. "Don't try to trick me, young woman." She grabbed the shirt and began stabbing the needle through it. "Fine. All right. I'll go to the doctor. Tomorrow. Now is anyone going to bring me some tea?"

"I will, Aunt Kate." No one could have missed the relief in Sarah's voice. She smiled at Addy and left the room, returning a few minutes later with cups and a pot full of tea.

An hour later, Addy relayed the events to Ma as they put dinner on the table.

"So she is for certain going to see Dr. Stephens tomorrow?" Ma asked.

"Yes, ma'am. She gave her word before I left."

"I wonder if I should go with her." The slight quake in Ma's voice revealed her concern.

"It might not hurt. At least you could talk to the doctor and find out exactly what's wrong." It would be like Aunt Kate to keep any news to herself that she didn't want anyone to know.

Addy was in bed with the light out before she realized she hadn't thought any more about Jim Castle or working at the hunting lodge or running away on a train. She gave a low chuckle. Everything she needed was right here at home.

But Jim Castle's beguiling smile invaded her thoughts. In her fantasy world, she watched breathlessly as he rode up on his black stallion, moonlight streaming down on his jet-black hair. He gazed down at her, an inviting smile on his lips and a dangerous light in his eyes. Then the light darkened and his eyes smoldered. Slowly she nodded, and he reached down and swung her up behind him. She threw her arms around his waist and laid her head on his broad back, feeling the muscles ripple beneath his shirt. They rode away into the night.

She gasped. What was she thinking? Besides, she couldn't even get her fantasies right. His hair was more dark brown than black.

Groaning, she flopped over onto her stomach and pulled her pillow over her head. But just before sleep claimed her, a thought drifted through her mind. What would it be like to ride away with Jim and see the world?

eight

Nineteen heads bowed over books or tablets as Addy cleaned the blackboard and then began writing the assignments for the next day. Thankfully the children were behaving extra well today. With thoughts of riding off in the moonlight with Jim Castle continuing to rattle her, interspersed with worry about Aunt Kate, she wasn't sure how she'd handle an unruly classroom.

When she'd finished, she turned and sat at her desk. One by one, the children closed their books or laid pencils on the desk and looked at her expectantly. She placed a finger to her lips as a reminder that some were still busy with their lessons.

When little Charlotte Greene took a deep breath and laid her pencil down, Addy smiled at the class. "Everyone finished?"

Heads bobbed in the affirmative; eyes shone with expectation.

"I'm so proud of how well you've all done on our class project. With the end-of-school program just a week away, I'm sure you'll all work hard to do your part to make it special for your families." She smiled at the serious expressions of the younger children as they nodded.

From the back of the room, Tom Schuyler, one of the older boys, raised his hand.

"Yes, Tom?"

"My pa says if you don't let us out of school soon, he's gonna take me out anyway. He needs me on the farm."

"I know, Tommy. Your father spoke to me yesterday, and I explained to him that we were running a little longer this year because of the heavy snows last winter." She sent him a reassuring smile. "He said another week would be fine."

Several hands shot up.

"Class, I've talked to each of your parents about the delay, and they all agreed they could manage without your help for another week." She wished they'd chosen to inform their children of that fact.

All the hands went down except one.

"Yes, Johnny?"

"Teacher, guess what the train brung in yesterday?" His grin just about split his face, and his freckles seemed to stand out against his face.

A cacophony of voices roared across the room.

"Children, children, please be quiet." She stood until all the voices had ceased. "Brought, Johnny."

"Yes, ma'am. You know what the train brought?" He stressed the last word, his eyes sparkling.

"Why don't you tell us?" She was pretty sure she knew but wouldn't mind confirmation.

"All the parts of a broken-down old building. They brung . . .brought it all the way from St. Louis." He took a deep breath. "Guess what they're gonna do with the stuff?"

Once more hands waved in the air.

"Philip, do you know the answer to Johnny's question?" It wouldn't do to let the boy be the center of attention every moment.

"Yes, ma'am." Philip, who walked with a limp due to a birth defect, smiled. "A group of businessmen bought the State of Maine Exhibition Building that was at the World's Fair. They took it apart and brought it here. When they reassemble it, they'll turn it into a hunting lodge."

So, it was true. The butterflies in Addy's stomach flitted and zoomed.

"Can we all go there?" Annie hadn't bothered to raise her hand, but Addy couldn't blame her. The news was exciting.

Carl twisted in his seat and frowned. "No, dummy, I mean,

sorry, Miss Sullivan, no, Annie. Only rich people will be allowed in."

"How did you manage to get that bit of information, Carl?" Addy could well imagine it would have come from his father.

"My pa said so. He said only rich folks could afford to go there."

"I see. Well, we'll have to wait and find out if your father is correct, won't we?" she said. "And now, I think we have just enough time to go over your lines for the program. If you'll all come to the front of the room we'll go through the play from beginning to end."

With help from several of the older students, Addy had written a short play for some of the children to perform that told the story of transportation and shipping in the area, beginning with horses, oxen, wagons, ferries, and riverboats, then ending with several students playing the parts of the officials of the White River Line. At the end of the play, the entire class would sing a lively rendition of "The Levee Song," also called "I've Been Working on the Railroad." Afterward the parents would view the illustrated essay the class had put together about the first train to arrive at the Branson Depot.

Addy's heart raced as the children rehearsed their parts. She chuckled. If she was this proud and nervous for them, she could only imagine how their parents would feel. A few of them stumbled over their lines, but Addy felt sure all would go well for the actual program the following week.

"That's wonderful, children. Please line up at the door."

After dismissing the children, Addy stepped outside and locked the door. Bobby was waiting beside her horse and buggy. She smiled and gave him his money, then waved as he walked away beaming.

She patted the dappled horse on the nose, climbed into her buggy, and sat for a moment, indecision coursing through her. She should hurry home to find out what the doctor had said about Aunt Kate. But would it hurt to swing by the bluff on which the new lodge would be built? Not for long, just to see if any activity was going on yet?

She licked her lips. It would only take a few extra minutes, fifteen or twenty at the most, to drive over that way, take a quick look, and drive back. Addy picked up the reins. With a flick of her wrist and a click of her tongue, she turned her buggy toward the river bluff.

Rough shouts of laughter reached her ears as she drew near her destination. She pulled on the reins and stopped in the middle of the narrow, rocky road. Perhaps this wasn't such a good idea, but she'd stay out of sight and just take a quick look.

Taking a deep breath, she urged her horse on. She stopped at the edge of a large clearing. Someone must have been working here for some time. The last time she'd been in this part of Branson thick woods reached almost to the bluff overlooking the river.

Several brawny men hauled beams on their shoulders; others pounded huge nails into what looked like parts of walls. Addy gasped as one man yanked his shirt off and threw it on the ground. Backing up, she turned the buggy and hurried the horse back toward town, her heart thumping wildly.

What had possessed her to come up here? She should have known there would be a lot of rough men working. She should have waited until the lodge was constructed, and then she could have made inquiries. She groaned. Inquiries about what? There she went again. She absolutely would never go to work in a hunting lodge.

As she neared a bend in the road, a horse and rider appeared. She pulled up. Jim Castle. She glanced around to see if there was anywhere she could hide her horse and buggy before he spotted her.

But his horse quickened its pace, and Jim stopped beside her, bewilderment on his face.

⁊

Jim stared at Addy. What in the world was she doing up here?

Her face was flaming red and her hands trembled.

He tightened his lips. There was no telling what she'd seen or heard. The construction crew on this job was a pretty rowdy bunch. He should have warned her, but how was he to imagine she'd have a reason to come up here? Dismounting, he hurried over to her side. "My dear, are you all right?"

She glared at him for a moment. Then suddenly the red washed from her face, and she paled. Her face crumpled and tears pooled in her blue eyes.

Jim patted her hand, his heart pounding. Had someone accosted her? He rushed to the other side of the buggy and climbed up. Reaching over, he pulled her into his arms and patted her shoulder while she cried.

Suddenly she jerked her head up, almost slamming into his chin. "Someone needs to tell those ruffians not to. . .not to. . . disrobe in public."

"Disrobe?" Jim stared at her, horrified at what she might have seen.

"Yes. He took his shirt off and threw it on the ground, right there in front of everyone."

Relief washed over him. The men often got overheated and tossed their shirts aside, working in their undershirts. Still, to an innocent young lady it may have seemed scandalous. "I am so sorry, Addy. I'll speak to the foreman immediately."

"Thank you, Jim," she whispered. She swabbed her eyes with her frilly white handkerchief then blew her nose daintily. She breathed in a little sigh and smiled. "I'm perfectly all right, Jim."

"You're sure?"

"Yes, I am. I'm going home now."

"I wanted to let you know how much I enjoyed the picnic with your family. I'd like to repay you by taking you out to dinner, but there isn't really a nice eating establishment in town other than the Branson Hotel. Would you do me the honor some evening soon?"

"No, no. Not the hotel," she said.

A surge of disappointment shot through him.

"I have a better idea. Why don't you come to church Sunday then join us for dinner?"

Jim couldn't keep the grin off his face. "Are you sure it'll be all right with your folks?"

"Of course. Ma always cooks extra just in case."

"In that case, I'd be delighted."

A gust of wind swirled around them, and the sky suddenly clouded. Addy shivered.

"Perhaps I should put the top up on your buggy in case it should rain."

"Thank you. That would be nice." She smiled, lowering her lashes. "I'll expect to see you at church on Sunday then."

❧

Addy smiled all the way home, the memory of the bare-chested man lost in the memory of Jim's concern and care for her. He must not have minded that she'd talked so much when he drove her home from the picnic. She was so silly to have worried so.

She drove into the barn to put the horse and buggy away. The wagon was gone. Pa must have gone into town.

When she stepped into the house, she was met with an unnatural quiet, and no delicious aromas greeted her. Ma must not have started supper yet. She walked into the kitchen and saw a note propped up on the table.

She scanned it quickly, her heart fluttering. Aunt Kate. Not taking time to change from her school clothing, she rushed back out to the barn and once more harnessed the horse to the buggy.

She fought the urge to run the horse all the way to Aunt Kate's house. By the time she reached the Rayton farm, her bottom lip was cut from her teeth clamping down on it. Jumping down, she flung the reins over the porch rail and ran inside.

Aunt Sarah, seated on the sofa in the parlor, looked up, her face white.

Betty jumped up from the floor where she'd been playing with her dolls. She threw her arms around Addy's legs. "Addy, Mama and Papa had to go away with Uncle Will and Aunt Kate to the hospital."

Addy reached down and lifted her little sister. "I know, sweetheart. It's okay. They'll be home as soon as they can. And we'll wait here for them. Betty dear, I'm going to help Aunt Sarah cook some supper. If you'll stay here and play for a while, I'll let you help set the table."

"Okay." She returned to her dolls, holding them on her lap and speaking softly to them.

Sarah got up and followed Addy into the kitchen.

Addy placed her hands on Sarah's shoulders. "What's wrong with Aunt Kate?"

Sarah burst out crying. "They think it's her heart."

Heaviness sat on Addy's heart as they fixed supper and fed the children.

"Addy, if they aren't back by bedtime, could you and Betty sleep here?"

"Of course. I doubt I'll be able to sleep anyway until we know something."

nine

After tossing and turning for hours, Addy sat on the side of the bed, her head in her hands. Her skin and nightgown were damp, from either her nervousness or the warm night. She had to get some rest. Otherwise, how would she be able to teach, much less keep order in her classroom, the next day?

Betty whimpered and kicked at her covers, which had become twisted around her legs.

Addy got up and walked around to her sister's side of the bed and rearranged the light covers, tucking them up around Betty's chest.

Addy stood for a moment, trying to decide whether to give the elusive sleep another chance. Maybe a glass of water would help.

She tiptoed into the kitchen so as not to awaken Sarah and the children. Moonlight streamed into the room from the window over the washstand, lighting her way. She stood for a moment, looking across the backyard. The leaves on the oak trees moved slightly, and a trace of a breeze sifted through the open window, touching her damp skin. She shivered.

After she'd filled a glass, she walked toward the front of the house. She grabbed a light shawl from the stand by the door and stepped onto the front porch. Aunt Kate's wicker rocking chair seemed to send an invitation and she sat. Leaning her head back, she shivered as the breeze brushed across her damp skin.

The rattle of harness and the *clip-clop* of hooves startled her, and she jerked awake, confused. She twisted her neck to loosen the tight muscles. Suddenly aware of the sound that had awakened her, she jumped to her feet, wrapping the shawl around her shoulders for modesty.

Uncle Will's two-seater open carriage came into view, the horses' coats shining in the moonlight. Addy peered anxiously. Then relief washed over her. Aunt Kate sat beside Ma in the back seat. Uncle Will pulled alongside the steps and got out then reached to help Aunt Kate. She stumbled a little as her foot touched the ground, but Uncle Will quickly steadied her. Addy took her great-aunt's other arm as Pa helped Ma down from the buggy.

Addy bit her lip as Aunt Kate wobbled a little. "Are you all right, Aunt Kate?"

"I'm fine, as I told everyone I was. Just tired."

"Aunt Kate." Sarah appeared in the doorway, her wrapper pulled snug around her waist and her hair hanging loose around her shoulders. "Are you all right?"

"Yes, yes, child. I'm fine. I need a nice cup of hot tea. Then I'm going to bed."

"Yes, ma'am. I'll get it right away." She rushed toward the kitchen.

When Aunt Kate was ensconced on the settee in the parlor, Addy seated herself next to her and took her hand, throwing Ma a questioning look.

Ma gave an imperceptible shake of her head.

Soon Sarah was back with the laden tray. Addy helped her hand out the cups, and Sarah poured. Pa made a face as he quickly drained his cup. He always preferred a strong cup of black coffee.

Uncle Will, Ma, and Pa talked quietly of their trip to Springfield for a few minutes, and then Ma helped Aunt Kate to bed. Addy slipped away to get dressed.

When she returned to the parlor, Ma smiled. "She fell asleep almost as soon as she laid down."

"I'll hitch up the wagon and pull it around, then come in and get Betty so we can go home," Pa said and left the room.

"Ma."

"Wait, Addy." Ma turned to Sarah. "I'll let Will tell you what the doctor said, but I'll be over in the morning after I stop by Rafe and Abby's to let them know what's going on. We'll talk then."

Sarah nodded, concern in her eyes. "I'll have a pot of coffee ready."

A few minutes later, Addy climbed into the back of the wagon, seating herself on a pile of quilts and stretching her legs out. Pa laid Betty beside her, gently placing her head in Addy's lap.

As soon as they started down the lane, Addy blurted out, "Please tell me about Aunt Kate. Is it her heart?"

Ma turned on her seat, and the sadness in her eyes answered the question even before she spoke. "Yes, dear. Her heart is giving out. The doctors said she needs to slow down. They don't want her even doing housework for now or outside chores."

"But. . .is she dying?" Addy's mind could hardly wrap itself around the thought. Aunt Kate had been so full of life for as long as she'd known her.

Pain crossed Ma's face. "The doctor didn't say how long she has, Addy. I think a lot of it depends on how well she follows orders."

Addy sighed. Aunt Kate wasn't likely to voluntarily sit back and do nothing. "Well, we'll just have to make her follow them."

Ma's brow wrinkled as she gave a little nod. "Honey, you need to remember she's not a young woman anymore."

"I know, Ma." Addy's voice broke, and she fought back the tears she'd been holding in for hours. Aunt Kate had been in her fifties when Ma and Uncle Will had come to live with their father's older sister. That was more than thirty years ago. "I'm so sorry, Ma. I know how much you love her."

Ma nodded, her eyes swimming, and turned back around on the wagon seat.

"Ma, would you like for me to ride over to Abby and Rafe's before I go to school in the morning?" That not only would save her mother time but would also keep her from having to tell the sad news once more.

"Yes, if you're sure you have time. I wouldn't want you to be late." The relief in Ma's voice was obvious.

"I could take Betty over there if you want me to. I know Abby wouldn't mind watching her while you go over to Uncle Will's."

"That might be a good idea, Lexie," Pa said. "That way she won't have to go out to the field with me."

Addy leaned back against the side of the wagon and let her silent tears flow.

❧

Jim laughed as one of the twin boys grabbed Rafe around the knees.

"Take me, Papa. Take me." The toddler chortled, holding tight.

"Now, Dawson"—Rafe leaned over and gently removed the child's arms from his leg—"I told you, you can't go to the field with me today. I have too much work to do."

Dawson's chin quivered as he attempted to hold back tears. "But I help."

As Rafe spoke softly to the child, Jim couldn't help but grin at the change in his friend over the last few years. He turned at the sound of horses approaching. His heart thundered inside his chest at the sight of Addy.

Rafe stood, holding Dawson in his arms while Jim lifted tiny Betty from the buggy then helped Addy to alight.

"Betty honey, why don't you take Dawson and Davie to their room and tell them a story while I talk to Rafe and Abby."

"Okay, but her name's really Tuck, you know." Betty took the hand of the little boy whom Rafe had deposited on the porch, and they went inside.

"What's wrong, sis?"

Jim glanced at his friend. He'd never heard Rafe speak so tenderly to Addy before. Usually he just teased her.

"Oh Rafe, it's Aunt Kate." Her face crumpled, and she fought back tears.

Jim took a step toward her but stopped when Rafe put an arm around her and led her toward the door. Jim wanted nothing but to go with them, to wrap his arms around Addy and shield her from whatever was causing her grief. But he hadn't the right. He took a deep breath.

"I'll wait out here," he said.

Rafe nodded, but Addy stopped and gave him an almost pleading look. "No, please come inside with us."

"Of course." Mixed feelings battled within him. Sorrow and fear at whatever was causing Addy's pain but joy that she wanted him with her.

When they stepped inside, Abby came from the kitchen wiping her hands on her apron. "Addy, what are you doing here this time of day?"

"It's Aunt Kate. There's something wrong with her heart." She reached both arms out to her sister, and they held each other tightly.

"Come into the parlor and sit down. Tell me everything."

Jim frowned as Addy told them the news about her great-aunt.

Abby jumped up, her face white. "I'm going over there right now. Maybe she'll listen to me. I'm not ready to let her go."

Rafe took his wife's hand and pulled her gently back down beside him. "Sweetheart, calm down. You can't go over there in this state."

Addy took her sister's other hand. "I don't know yet just how bad it is. Ma was too upset to talk much. But she needs to go over and check on Aunt Kate and talk to Sarah and Will, probably about Aunt Kate's care. I really need you to stay here and keep Betty while I'm at school. Would you mind?"

Abby let out a long, slow breath. "All right, I will. But as soon as you pick her up, I'm going."

Addy stood and placed a hand on her sister's shoulder. "Try not to worry too much. Ma didn't say she was going to die, just that she had to slow down. Remember last year, when Mr. Wilkins started having heart problems? His daughters all thought he was dying, but he's doing fine."

"That's right." Abby perked up. "He played three games of horseshoes at the last church picnic."

Jim watched in amazement at the composure on Addy's face. She'd calmed down not only her sister but herself as well. Jim followed her out onto the porch. "I'm heading into town, too. Would you mind if I ride along beside you?"

Relief crossed her face. "I'd be grateful. To be honest, I'd just as soon not be alone with my thoughts."

He mounted Finch and kept his pace with Addy's. They rode in silence for a few moments, and then Addy sighed.

Jim groped in his mind for something to say to get her mind off her aunt's condition.

"I don't believe I've ever seen so much honeysuckle growing in one area." Great, talk about flowers.

"I know." She threw him a pensive smile. "I've always loved the aroma. Even better than lilacs, I believe."

Well, if talking about flowers would make her feel better, that's what he'd do. "Have you ever smelled magnolia blossoms?"

"No, I don't believe I have." She glanced up, her blue eyes wide. "They grow on trees, don't they?"

"Yes, and mostly down south. The blossoms have a sweet, lemony smell."

She giggled. "Sweet? Lemony? Lemons don't smell sweet."

He laughed. "Maybe I should have said lemonade."

"Or lemon pie," she said with a teasing grin.

"Or lemon soda," he said, picking up the game.

"Do magnolia trees grow very big?"

"Some of them are very large. And the leaves are deep velvety, satiny green."

"Now there you go again. How can they be satin and velvet at the same time?" Her lips puckered in an amused smile, and he wanted nothing more than to bend over and press his own against their softness.

"You're absolutely right." He wondered if his voice sounded as shaky to her as it did to him. "I need to get my facts straight before attempting to teach a teacher."

They arrived in front of the school laughing. Jim dismounted and held his hand out to her. As she placed her soft hand into his rough paw, his throat constricted, and he swallowed past what felt like a lump.

She looked up into his eyes and smiled. "Thank you for getting my mind off Aunt Kate for a while. It wouldn't do for me to be in tears all day while I'm trying to teach."

"It was my pleasure, Addy." He lifted her hand and brushed his lips across their softness.

"Have a pleasant day, my dear." He stood and watched as she entered the building. Then he mounted his horse and headed toward the hunting lodge construction site.

ten

Would the man ever get to the point? Addy cringed at her disrespect as Reverend Smith's voice droned on and on. But really. If her nerves hadn't been on edge from being sandwiched between her mother and Jim, she was sure she'd have nodded off to sleep by now. She fanned her fingers in front of her face. It didn't do anything for the hot air, but at least it kept her from yawning.

The sermon was on mutual respect in the family and should have been interesting and helpful, but Addy was hard put not to squirm.

Wait. What was he saying? *No, oh please, God, don't let him read from Song of Solomon. Not with Jim Castle seated next to me.*

" 'Behold, thou art fair, my love; behold, thou art fair; thou hast doves' eyes within thy locks: thy hair is as a flock of goats. . . .'"

Chapter four. He was reading from chapter four. Addy's mind tore through the chapter she had thought so beautiful in her private Bible readings. Oh no. Surely he wouldn't continue. She gasped as he continued through verse four.

A movement beside her drew her attention. Jim was shaking. Was he laughing at her?

In spite of her embarrassment, she threw him a look that she hoped would show him what she thought of his inappropriate amusement.

"Well, I won't go on because I don't want to offend any of our ladies, but the Song of Solomon reveals Christ's love for the church, and as we are told in Ephesians 5:25, 'Husbands, love your wives, even as Christ also loved the church, and gave himself for it.'"

Addy let out a breath she hadn't realized she was holding and focused on Reverend Smith's face in an attempt to avoid Jim's.

As soon as the final benediction had been said, Addy stood and followed Ma out, conscious of Jim crowding her from behind.

When she stepped outside the old log building into the sunshine, she inhaled deeply of the fresh air.

Jim stepped up beside her. She glared at him but nevertheless took his proffered arm.

Ma turned to Jim with a huge smile. "We're so pleased you are coming to dinner, Mr. Castle."

"Thank you, ma'am. And I'm honored to have been invited, but I assure you, I'll understand if you want to make it another time. I realize Miss Rayton's illness is a worry for you." He returned her smile.

"Actually Aunt Kate is doing very well. She's even following doctor's orders and is feeling much better." Ma's voice rang with relief.

They'd all been surprised when Aunt Kate rallied a couple of days after her visit to the doctor. Addy wondered if the doctor had given them a false diagnosis. She couldn't help the hope that rose in her at the thought.

"I'm very happy to hear that. And since that is the case, I will be delighted to accept that invitation." He hesitated before adding, "I hope you don't mind if I offer Addy a ride to your home."

"I don't mind at all. You two run right along. We'll see you there." She climbed into the carriage beside Pa and Betty, and the next thing Addy knew she was standing beside Jim, quite alone.

"Addy, I'm so sorry that I offended you when I laughed. I don't know what came over me."

She narrowed her eyes at him. He seemed sincere. Perhaps he really hadn't intended to laugh, although what he could have possibly thought was funny was beyond her. "Very well, Mr. Castle. I think I can overlook your indiscretion just this once."

"I'm deeply grateful, but it's Jim, remember?"

She took a deep breath and blew it out with a gush. "Oh, all right, Jim."

As they rode down the lane toward the farm, Jim glanced at her. "How about going for a drive this afternoon?"

"A drive where, in particular?"

"Oh, I haven't been to Marble Cave since I've been back in town."

She wrinkled her nose. "Why do you want to go there? I've always hated that dirty cave."

"We wouldn't need to go inside the cave. I'd sort of like to say hello to the Lynch family."

"I suppose that would be all right. I haven't visited with the Lynch sisters in ages." She threw him a teasing glance. "But don't think you'll change my mind about going inside that cave. Because you won't."

"I wouldn't dream of it. He grinned and clicked to the horse that'd slowed to a walk. Within a few minutes they were pulling alongside the Sullivans' porch.

Addy turned toward the door, and Jim placed his hand on her arm. "You're really going to have to stop jumping down by yourself. How will I ever convince you I'm a gentleman if you won't even allow me to help you from a carriage?"

She blushed but remained in her seat until he came around to help her down.

After leaving Jim in the parlor with Pa, Addy went to the kitchen to help her ma, who was dishing up summer squash and stewed tomatoes into serving bowls. A platter filled with slices of sizzling fried ham stood on the kitchen table.

Addy washed her hands and donned an apron. "I'll set the table."

"Ma already set the table," Betty announced. "And I helped.

And I took the preserves and pickled peaches in, too."

Addy gave her little sister a smile and planted a kiss on her head. "You're getting to be such a big girl, Bets, and a real help to Ma."

Betty nodded, a proud grin on her face. "That's what Pa said, too."

Addy wondered, not for the first time, why Ma and Pa waited so long to have a child. Addy and her sister were nearly twenty-one when Betty was born. So Ma Lexie would have been close to forty. Of course, it couldn't have been easy, starting their married life with two nine-year-old orphan girls. She wondered if that was why they'd waited. She'd never had the nerve to ask the personal question. "Well then, I'll start carrying the food into the dining room, Ma."

"Oh, thank you, dear. The bread will be nice and warm in just a moment."

A few minutes later, Addy surveyed the laden table. She straightened a napkin or two then went to the parlor to call Pa and Jim to dinner.

Jim looked up as she entered the room, and as their eyes met, butterflies did a flip-flop in Addy's stomach. He stood and offered his arm.

When she placed her hand on his forearm, a tingle began in her fingers, and by the time they arrived at the table, it had reached her heart.

❧

She felt it, too. He could tell by the look on her face. It wasn't his imagination. On the other hand, her obvious embarrassment that had begun with the minister's sermon seemed to be growing worse, and his heart ached for her. He simply must do something to get her mind off it.

"Jack, it's come to my attention you were a riverboat captain at one time." Oops. That might not be the best topic since she was the one who told him about her father's previous occupation.

A light came into Jack's eyes. "Yes, as a matter of fact, I was. I captained the *Julia Dawn* for a number of years."

"That must have been exciting. Ever come across river pirates?" Of course not. The man wasn't that old. River piracy had pretty much come to an end before the mid-1800s.

Jack gave him a curious look, and then his glance flitted to Addy. He turned his attention back to Jim, understanding in his eyes. "No, the river pirates' day had ended before my first cabin boy job. But I knew an old galley cook who could tell some hair-raising stories about when he was a lad on the river.

Addy's eyes came alive with excitement. "Do you mean Pap Sanders?"

"That's right. Pap was getting up there in years by the time I signed on as a cabin boy. He almost made me wish I'd been born back in the days of the river pirates." A hearty chuckle exploded from his lips. "Of course, youngsters don't have a lot of sense."

"He didn't tell Tuck and me about any river pirates. I mean Abby and me."

"Because I threatened him within an inch of his life if he so much as mentioned the word in your presence." Jack smiled at her then looked at Betty, who stared at him, wide eyed. He gave her a wink then turned to Jim. "Which reminds me there is a child at the table. We'd best continue this conversation later."

"Of course," Jim said. "Did you grow up around here, sir?"

Jack didn't answer for a moment. Then he nodded. "I lived in this house with my uncle for four years after my parents died. I didn't have much use for it then. Or anything else for that matter. I took off when I was sixteen. Signed on with the first steamboat I came across that would hire me."

His eyes rested on his wife, and they exchanged warm smiles. "It was years before I learned to love this place. I miss the river now and then, but I've never regretted selling out.

Farming is in my blood now, and I love it as much as or more than I ever loved my life up and down the river."

Jim was almost embarrassed to be witnessing the love between Jim and Lexie. What would it be like to come home to a wife and children who loved him? He swallowed past the lump that suddenly clogged his throat. What was the matter with him? It wasn't like him to be sentimental. But he couldn't deny the longing that had sprung up inside.

He cleared his throat and took a bite of squash, relishing the buttery taste. It was good to get some home cooking. And the fried ham slices were about the best he'd ever tasted. Almost as good as the fried chicken at the picnic. He wondered if Addy would ever learn to fry chicken like that.

Realizing the direction his thoughts were headed, he scrambled around for something to say to get his mind off marriage to Addy. "Mrs. Sullivan, you're a wonderful cook. I can't remember ever eating ham that tasted this good."

A pleased blush washed over her cheeks. "Why thank you, Mr. Castle. I do believe you said the same thing about my fried chicken at the picnic. I'm very pleased that you like my cooking."

After the meal, Addy and her mother began clearing the table.

"Jim, Let's go sit on the front porch and let our food settle," Jack suggested.

"Sounds good to me." Jim followed him outside where they sat on cane-bottomed chairs. "Did you make these?"

Jack grinned. "Wish I could take credit, but I never had the patience to learn the craft. Rafe's pa makes them. His pa taught him, and I guess his pa's pa and on up the line. I also have a couple of horsehair chairs he made."

Jim shook his head. "I think I saw a couple of those at Rafe's house."

"Yes, it's going to be a lost art before long. The younger folks want fancy store-bought furniture and don't appreciate the beauty and the love that goes into these."

"Or the time."

"Or the time," Jack echoed.

The door opened and Addy stepped onto the porch. "Oh, blessed relief," she said. "It feels nice out here."

Jack stood and stretched. "Well, I think I'll take my Sunday afternoon snooze. I guess you two can keep each other company."

"I guess we can, Pa," Addy said. "Enjoy your rest. We might go over to Marble Cave. Let Ma know so she won't worry about where I am." She gazed after him with a fond smile then sat in the chair he'd vacated.

"We don't have to go there if you don't want to, Addy. We could go for a ride by the river. It's probably cooler there."

"No, I don't mind. I'm sort of looking forward to seeing the Lynch girls." She giggled. "Although I don't think they could rightly be called girls, and neither one of them is a Lynch anymore."

He grinned but not at her words. What an enchanting little giggle. A ride by the river was sounding more and more pleasant. Too bad he'd mentioned the cave. Ah well, he wondered if the sight of the place would remind her of their first meeting.

eleven

Addy leaned back in the buggy seat, enjoying the summer greenery as they passed through the narrow tree-lined road. Addy was surprised to see at least a dozen buggies in the clearing by the cave in addition to a number of saddle horses. She hadn't realized the Lynches were this busy.

As they pulled up in front of the Marble Cave office, a sense of familiarity surged through her. She didn't think she'd come here since Abby married. And she'd only been here a couple of times before that. Once to hear her sister and the old men in her band.

Did Abby miss playing the violin in public? She said she didn't, but she sure didn't turn down any chance to play for the family or church programs. There was no denying Abby had talent. With the proper training, there was no telling how far she could have gone.

As they got out of the buggy, Mr. Lynch came forward, a huge grin on his face. He grabbed Addy's hand in both of his huge ones. "Tuck Collins! It's about time you came to see me."

Addy laughed. "Sorry, sir. I'm not Tuck. I'm her twin sister, Addy Sullivan."

Consternation crossed his face. "Oh. Miss Sullivan, forgive me. I never could tell you two apart. Except when Tuck was wearing her overalls." His jovial voice boomed.

She retrieved her hand, which was growing numb in his tight clasp. "That's quite all right, Mr. Lynch," she said. "It's a common mistake." Though not as often since Addy had been teaching school in town.

The two men shook hands, and Mr. Lynch said, "What brings you today, Jim?"

"I mainly wanted to see the place for old time's sake." As organ music bellowed from the cave, Jim darted a glance in that direction. "What's going on in the cave?"

"Ah, a wedding today. A young couple from Forsyth thought it would be romantic to get married in the Cathedral Room. After the ceremony, you should take a look at how well my girls decorated the cavern." He spoke with pride, and Addy knew it was well deserved. The Lynch sisters were known for their talents in music and decorating. "They're also providing the music. My youngest is playing the organ, and the oldest sang a special song. I wish you could've heard her sing." He kissed his lips to his fingers in appreciation.

"I've heard her sing many times, Mr. Lynch, at community socials," Addy said. "It's something I always look forward to. She has such a lovely voice."

"Ah yes, Miss Sullivan, and your sister is very talented, too. Tell her I miss her fiddle very much."

"I will." Addy smiled and glanced at Jim. He held out his arm, and she laid her hand on it, relieved he was ready to go.

"If you don't mind, sir, I'd like to take Addy for a stroll."

She groaned inwardly. The sooner she got away from the cave, the happier she'd be.

They strolled through a wooded area then walked up a path until they stood on a bluff overlooking the cave.

"Isn't this the site of the old mining town?"

"Yes, Marmoros." He shook his head. "I've heard it was a fairly wild place before it burned down."

Addy nodded. "It didn't just burn down. The Baldknobbers did it deliberately, or so they say."

"Yes, I heard that, too." He frowned. "I wonder why they did it."

She shrugged. "Who knows? From what I've heard, they wanted to control everything. They didn't want the town here for some reason. And it seems they got their way."

Sudden nostalgia gripped her. "Actually that was the night I first met Ma Lexie."

"Really?"

"Yes. You see, Papa Jack had taken Abby and me in a few days before." She gave him a side grin. "Well, actually, we were camping out in his house when he came home from a trip down the river. He found us and didn't know what to do with us."

Interest washed over his face, and he laughed. "I'd like to hear all of that story."

"Maybe someday," she said with a smile. "But to go on with this story, Papa Jack smelled smoke and finally saw flames coming from Marmoros. He told us to stay in the house and took off on his horse. About an hour later, we were just about to go looking for him when Ma and Uncle Will showed up with Pa all wounded. At first we thought he was dead."

"That must have been frightening."

"It was. When we saw he was alive but unconscious, we figured they might take us to an orphanage, so we pretended Jack was our Pa. Boy did that lie cause a lot of trouble for everyone." She still felt guilt over that every now and then.

"So your parents met here by Marble Cave," he said with an odd look on his face.

"Well, so to speak. They actually saw each other once before in Forsyth."

"You and I met here, too, you know," he said. "I think you've forgotten."

"Here?" She searched her memories. "No, Jim. We met at Abby and Rafe's wedding, remember?"

"Think back, Addy. Remember the day Abby came to apply for the temporary job for her band? Because the Lynch girls were going away on vacation?"

Suddenly light broke through the darkness. She remembered following Abby into the little office. Rafe had been there and. . .Jim! He was the one who took Abby's application. "Yes, I do remember now. I was in such a hurry to get away from the place, I couldn't think of anything else. I just knew Abby would try to talk me into entering the cave."

"You were wearing a blue dress with lace on the sleeves and collar," he said. "And you had a blue ribbon in your hair."

"Fancy you remembering that." How could he have carried around such a momentary memory for all this time? Even to remembering what she was wearing?

"It was easy for me to remember, Addy. You were and still are the most beautiful girl I've ever seen."

☙

Jim watched as varying emotions washed over Addy's face. Had he said too much? Would she think he was foolish? Or worse still, could he have been wrong to think she was beginning to return his feelings? That would make him as pathetic as the doctor.

He held his breath as a blush washed over her cheeks. She didn't appear to be angry or disgusted. If anything, she looked pleased. He took a deep breath as relief surged through him.

She cleared her throat. "Thank you. That's a very nice thing to say, although I'm sure you're only teasing me."

"My dear"—he took her hands, and she lowered her eyes—"I mean every word of it."

"Thank you," she whispered then gently removed her hands from his. "But perhaps we should go now."

"Of course." He led her down the steep pathway toward the cave, where the wedding party was ascending from the enormous Cathedral Room below. He hoped the stairs had been replaced with something a little more fitting for formal clothing.

The bride and groom stood to one side shaking hands with their guests. Apparently they had no plans to run away from the crowd, at least not for the present.

Addy had paused, and when Jim looked at her, her eyes were focused on the bride. Her hand resting on his arm trembled. She darted a look up at him, and when she realized he was watching her, she blushed once more.

He helped her into the buggy and started down the road toward her home. Wanting to put her at ease, he smiled. "If you have no objection and no other plans, I'd like to take you to dinner at the Branson Hotel next week. After all, I've accepted your family's hospitality several times."

Suddenly she looked straight into his eyes. "I have no objections at all."

He grinned at her sudden transformation from shyness to honesty. "In that case, will you marry me?"

"Oh, you. Don't be silly." She cast a captivating smile his way. "Don't get too sure of yourself. I've only agreed to dinner. I haven't said I'd marry you."

"Are you by any chance telling me to slow down?" He felt giddy as a girl from her new attitude toward him.

"Yes, indeed, Mr. Jim Castle." Suddenly the laughter slid from her face. "I would love to be your friend. Rafe and Abby have been best friends nearly all their lives. I believe friendship is very important in any relationship. Don't you agree?"

"I do agree. And since we're now discussing Rafe and Abby, does that mean you might marry me after all?"

"Oh! There you go teasing me." She pressed her lips together in an unsuccessful attempt to hide the smile that was teasing her lips. "Let's talk about something else."

"Very well. Your wish is my wish. What would you like to talk about?"

"I don't know." She was silent for a moment. "Oh, yes I do. Tell me about the new hunting lodge."

This girl never ceased to surprise him. "What do you want to know about it?"

"What sort of staff will they need? And will they be hiring local people?"

"Partly. They'll bring a management team from St. Louis. But they'll be hiring locals for bellboys and other serving and cleaning staff."

"Will they hire any women?"

"I'm sure they'll hire women for housekeeping."

"But not for the desk or serving?" Disappointment filled her eyes. Now what had she been thinking?

"Very unlikely. Since this will be a gentleman's lodge, they'll hire mostly male staff." He cut a glance at her, curious about the types of questions she was asking. "Why? Do you know someone who needs employment?"

"Oh, no, no. I was just curious, that's all." She frowned and looked away. "My, the honeysuckle does smell sweet."

Back to flowers again. "Yes, they do. Quite a heady smell, I'd say."

When they arrived at the farm, the family was sitting down to supper. Lexie insisted that Jim join them for ham sandwiches and potato salad left over from dinner.

Betty kept up a continuous round of questions directed at Jim, until finally her Pa told her that was quite enough and to stop being rude. With a pout, she said, "I'm sorry, Mr. Jim."

"That's quite all right, Miss Betty. I always enjoy the conversation of beautiful young ladies." He threw her a grin and a wink, and she giggled.

When he'd taken his last delicious bite of blackberry cobbler, Jim asked Jack if he could speak to him in private.

With a knowing look, Jack agreed, and they went onto the front porch.

As Jim drove toward town later, he couldn't help laughing at himself. He'd been as nervous as a gangling boy as he asked Jack for permission to court his daughter. And the nervousness didn't end there. Jack had shot question after question at Jim for at least a half hour.

The hard question he'd saved for last. "What are your

plans for the future?"

"Sir, I wish I could say we'd settle down here, but you know my job takes me all over the country. Sometimes out of the country."

"Does Addy know you intend to stay with your present job?"

Jim shook his head. "We haven't actually discussed that yet. But I promise I'll speak to her about it soon."

Jack nodded. "Make it very soon. Before you talk to her about courting. I won't have you courting her under false pretenses."

"I'm leaving for Kansas City tomorrow, but I promise I'll talk to her as soon as I get back. In fact, we're having dinner together next Sunday." He hastened to add, "Just as friends of course."

Finally Jack offered his hand and said he had no objection at all as long as Addy was agreeable as well.

As Jim rode into town, worry and a niggling doubt wormed their way into his thoughts. He'd finally settled it for himself that things could work out well, even if he was on the road a lot. She could travel with him most of the time.

But now he wasn't so sure. What if she wasn't willing? Maybe he shouldn't have been in such a hurry to talk to Jack.

twelve

Addy couldn't believe how much she missed seeing Jim around town. When she drove in each morning, her eyes automatically wandered to the Branson Hotel, although she knew he wouldn't be back until later in the week. When she left school in the afternoon, her vision roamed the area, searching for a sight of his tall form and broad shoulders.

He'd said good-bye Sunday night and told her he'd be gone most of the week but would try to be back in time for the children's program on Friday.

She wondered what he'd spoken to Pa about after dinner Sunday night. Could he have been asking to court her? But then, wouldn't he have said something? Or wouldn't Pa have? Unless Pa said no, but that wasn't likely. After all, this wasn't the Dark Ages, and a girl had a right to choose her own beau these days. If Pa had disapproved for some reason, he'd have still left the choice to her.

"Miss Sullivan, Johnny pulled my hair!" A screech from across the room drew Addy's attention back to her class.

She focused her gaze on the small culprit. "Johnny, go sit on the stool in the corner."

"Aw, Miss Sullivan, I'm sorry."

"I certainly hope you are sorry. Perhaps while you're in the corner you will consider how it feels to have someone yank on your hair. Then perhaps you will be truly sorry and can honestly apologize to Alice."

"Yes, ma'am." Johnny trudged to the punishing corner and perched on the stool, his back to the classroom.

"All right, class." She motioned to the class project hanging on the front wall. "Our project looks wonderful, and it's very

87

informative. All the individual pictures and essays will go on the wall tomorrow. We only have today and tomorrow to practice for our program. Friday, we'll have to get the classroom ready. No homework tonight. Is everybody happy?"

A chorus of "uh huhs" and "yes, ma'ams" thundered across the room.

Addy grinned and lifted her hand. "All right. Put your things away and line up."

"What about me?" Johnny wailed from his stool.

"You, too, Johnny. But I'd like for you to apologize to Alice for pulling her hair. And I'm not sure you've learned your lesson in ten minutes. So you will have to clean the blackboard the rest of this week."

Ten minutes later, she dismissed the children and gathered her own things together. She locked the door behind her and stood on the step for a moment, glancing toward the business section of town, finally resting her eyes on the luxury hotel down the street. Her heart raced, and she pictured herself seated across a cloth-covered table in a corner of the room. The lights would be turned down low.

Oh stop it, Addy. You'll be dining on Sunday afternoon in broad daylight.

With a shake of her head, she stepped into the dusty street. She spoke a few words to Bobby before handing him his coin then climbed into her buggy.

She sat for a moment, undecided about whether to ride over to see Aunt Kate or go straight home. Finally she drove to the Rayton farm and spent time with her great-aunt. She was pleased and relieved to see some color back in Aunt Kate's face.

"Mercy, child, don't you be worrying about me. I'm taking things slow just like the doctor said, and I'm feeling a lot better." Aunt Kate rocked back and forth slowly in her chair. "See? I'm even rocking slowly."

Addy laughed as she drove away an hour later. Restless

and on a sudden whim, she took the river road and drove to the family's favorite picnic spot. She got out and sat on a low bank, her feet almost touching the water.

Her thoughts went back to gliding past here on the deck of the *Julia Dawn*. She could almost hear the tinkling laughter of her and her sister as they ran and played above and below deck.

And good old Pap with his fiddle and his wild stories. It was true she'd never heard about the pirates from him, but she could remember shivering with fright as she and Abby huddled together on one of their bunks after a ghost story told on deck as the moon drifted behind the clouds. Of course Papa Jack never knew about it. He'd have raked Pap over the coals, but the girls would beg, and finally Pap would give in. She could still get goose bumps thinking about some of those old stories.

Her favorite times on the *Julia Dawn* were those mornings when they were allowed to get up early and watch the sun rise, its colorful rays peeping through the trees and reflecting on the water. The most beautiful sight she'd ever seen.

Someday she was going to board a steamboat and go down the river again. Of course, they were few and far between these days, and now that the White River Line was almost completed, they might disappear altogether. Anyway, it wouldn't be the same without Abby.

She scampered to her feet and climbed into the buggy. She was being silly. After all, she was a grown woman. It was time to put away childish thoughts of adventure.

She arrived home just in time to help Ma get supper on the table.

"How many days until the school program, sister?" Betty asked her this every day. The little girl was beside herself with excitement.

Addy smiled. "Just three more, Bets."

Betty jumped up and down, and Addy grabbed the plate

her sister was carrying just as it slipped from her hands. "Oh, Sorry, Addy. I'm so excited. I can't wait."

Addy laughed, "Me either. It's going to be a lot of fun, and you'll hear about adventures galore."

She looked fondly at her little sister's glowing face. Thank goodness Betty had years before she'd have to put aside her dreams of adventure.

☙

Jim opened the oversized menu with the star on the front. He'd had two invitations to dinner tonight but didn't feel like being around a lot of people. All he wanted to do was brood over Addy.

Dinner invitations weren't the only things he'd bowed out of. He'd turned down two more job offers this week. One group needed him next month, so that one had been easy to say no to, but the other, an exclusive New Orleans restaurant that had been losing its clientele, offered to wait until September in order to obtain his services. Jim knew he'd be finished here in Branson by then, but he didn't know if his situation with Addy would be settled. Would she be willing to leave Branson? He'd refused the offer. He could kick himself for not getting it settled before he'd left for Kansas City. He was afraid. That was the problem.

Maybe he should look around in Kansas City or St. Louis for a job. There wasn't any rule that said he had to keep doing what he was doing. Then they'd be close enough to visit Addy's family often. Not traveling all over the country. What had he been thinking? What kind of life was that for a woman?

The waiter came and took his order.

Jim took a long drink from his glass of ice water. Could he do it? Give up the career he'd built up over the past couple of years?

His steak arrived, but he'd lost his appetite. The porterhouse tasted like a slab of sawdust. Maybe it would have been better if he'd never taken the job in Branson.

❧

Addy breathed in the scent of the early summer afternoon as she drove her buggy up the lane toward Abby and Rafe's place. The kids had been high-strung today. She couldn't really blame them. They'd had a couple of accidents while gluing last-minute pictures on construction paper. But all ended well, and the walls of the room told the history of their hometown.

The children had been proud as they walked around the perimeter of the room and saw what they had accomplished. She hoped the parents would appreciate the labor of love they'd put into this project.

The final program practice had been a little rough, but she was sure the performance would go well. They knew their lines, and some of them were very good little actors and actresses.

In spite of all the busyness and excitement of the day, Addy had been restless. And for some reason, she had a strong urge to see Abby. She hoped her sister wasn't busy, but if she was, Addy would just pitch in and help her with whatever she was doing. They'd always worked well together.

Addy enjoyed the tomato canning season when she and Abby and Ma went to Aunt Kate's house and worked together to get tomatoes put up for the families and get others ready to sell to the tomato factory. It was always the highlight of the summer for Addy, in spite of the hard work.

But that was at least a month away. For now, she simply needed to see her sister's face and spend some time talking.

After three years, she should be used to Abby being gone, and she supposed it was easier than it used to be. But sometimes, like now, she missed her sister so much she simply needed that contact. She wondered if Abby felt the same. Probably not. After all, she had Rafe and their twin sons.

The farmhouse came into view, and Addy pulled up in front of the house, tying her horse loosely to the rail. She wouldn't be here that long, so no sense in unhitching him.

She tapped on the screen door and went on in. The aromas of fried pork chops and cooked apples tantalized her nostrils. "Abby?" she called out.

Abby's voice came from the kitchen. "I'm back here, sis."

Addy stepped into the kitchen and was greeted by four little arms encircling her legs.

"Aunt D, Aunt D." Their version of Aunt Addy.

She knelt down beside her nephews and gave them hugs, receiving sticky kisses in exchange.

"Uh oh. You boys have been scraping the apple bowl, haven't you?"

Abby laughed. "I always leave a little in there when I put them in to bake. For one thing, it keeps them occupied for a few minutes so I can get something done."

"You're very blessed, you know." Addy knew she sounded wistful and only hoped she didn't sound downright jealous."

Abby poured a cup of coffee and set it on the table. "Here, you look like you need this. And yes, I know I'm blessed."

Addy sat at the table while her sister washed the boys' faces and hands and then set them in the corner with their toys. Abby then sat across the table from Addy. "I'm glad you stopped by. Everything's okay, isn't it?" Abby scrutinized her twin's face.

"Yes, I just wanted to see you." Addy's eyes roamed to the boys again.

Abby reached over and placed a hand on Addy's. "You'll have children of your own one day, sis."

Addy nodded. "I hope so. I really do." She turned and looked at her twin. "Do you ever miss your old life? When you were with the band? And even before when we used to go with Papa Jack on the *Julia Dawn*?"

"Sure." Abby frowned a little. "I miss those things

sometimes. But I wouldn't give up my life with Rafe and my boys for anything."

Addy nodded. She wanted to tell Abby how torn she felt. Part of her yearned to settle down with a husband and babies, but another part wanted to hop on a train or a boat and explore the world. But she couldn't say that to Abby. Her sister would think she was losing her mind.

Maybe she was. One minute she was dreaming of Jim Castle asking for her hand in marriage, and the next her thoughts took her away to strange and new places.

How could she be so double-minded?

thirteen

Addy peeped out from behind the curtain hung to separate the actors from the rest of the room. She almost giggled at the sight of proud mamas seated on the small chairs that usually sat behind the students' desks. Johnny's mother had somehow managed to fit her portly body on one of the chairs, albeit squeezed tightly against Clara May's tiny bit of a mother on one side and Mrs. Marshall on the other. Ma and Addy perched on their chairs, with Betty on Ma's lap. At last year's Christmas party, Addy had planned to ask folks to bring chairs but was informed by several students that the parents always managed fine on the children's chairs and they probably wouldn't like it if she tried to change things.

Most of the men were lined up against the back wall, including Pa and Rafe, who each held one of the twins.

She scanned the room for Jim, but he hadn't yet arrived. Perhaps he wouldn't be back in time.

When it appeared that everyone was there who was coming, Addy stepped out and smiled at the crowd. "Ladies and gentlemen, we are so pleased you could come tonight. Your children have worked hard on this presentation, which depicts the history of transportation in our region. When the play is over, please feel free to look over the essays and pictures that are posted on the walls. The front wall from side to side is our joint project and tells the same story that you will see performed live. The other walls contain individual illustrated essays about the first train into Branson. These contain your children's own thoughts about the events of that day. We hope you will enjoy your evening. At this time, I'd like to introduce our narrator, Miss Annie Brown."

Hearty applause sounded across the room as fourteen-year-old Annie stepped out wearing a long, pioneer-type dress with an old-fashioned bonnet atop her head.

The curtain was pulled back, and Johnny and Sam, faces painted and dressed in buckskins, stepped in through the door. Each of the boys wore a band around his head with a feather sticking up proudly. With solemn looks on their faces, befitting the stalwart race they represented, each led an Indian pony across the front of the room while Annie told the story of the native population of Branson many years ago and their mode of transportation.

Whistles and clapping thundered through the schoolhouse as the boys led the ponies down the side aisle toward the front door. The effect of their solemn expressions was spoiled as they gave war cries while leading the ponies through the door.

Addy closed her eyes and shook her head while laughter exploded from the men. But she grinned and breathed a sigh of relief that there'd been no accidents. She hadn't relished the thought of cleaning up horse manure.

Next a small covered wagon made of cardboard and sheets rolled across the room. Two boys dressed up like oxen pulled the wagon along. No one seemed to mind that instead of four wheels, eight feet stuck out the bottom.

Addy, directing things, still managed to keep an eye out for Jim. The covered wagon had just made its way through the front door when his tall form stepped inside. His eyes searched the room until they spotted her. Addy attempted to keep her delight and excitement from her countenance, but when he grinned, she was pretty sure she hadn't succeeded.

She made it through the rest of the program without too many glances toward the back wall where he stood.

The final mode of transportation to be displayed was the students' pride and glory. A huge black engine made of cardboard chugged across the stage followed by two freight cars. The audience showed its approval of the train and the actors by whistles and applause.

When the train had made its way outside, Annie explained that as soon as the two ends of the White River Line met and connected, they would have passenger coaches as well.

The curtain was drawn again as all the students made their way back inside through the back door. Then it was pulled open, and with Addy on the piano, the class sang the closing song, "I've Been Working on the Railroad." When the chorus began for the second time, most of the audience members joined in.

Addy glanced at the crowd. From the proud looks on their faces and the jovial comments they made to one another, it was apparent the program was a huge success. Once more she reminded the guests not to leave before looking at the projects on the walls.

She glanced around for Jim. He stood reading one of the essays with a smile on his face. Her heart thumped. Of course he would find the essays interesting. He had interests in the railroad coming into Branson.

Suddenly a thought popped into her mind. She had no idea what those interests were. They had never really discussed what Jim did for a living. They always seemed to talk about her. She blushed. He must think she was terribly self-centered.

She pursed her lips. She was pretty sure it had something to do with the railroad. Didn't it? Oh dear, somehow she must turn their conversation to him when they spoke again. Or perhaps she should ask Abby. That way she wouldn't have to admit she didn't know anything about him except that he was handsome, he was Rafe's best friend, and he thought she was pretty.

She started as he appeared at her side. "Good evening, Jim."

"A very good evening," he said. "Your students are talented."

"Thank you. I think so, too. Fenton Taylor is a fine artist, and Annie Bolton writes very well."

"Yes, I saw her essay. She shows a lot of promise." He smiled into her eyes.

Addy fidgeted under his scrutiny. She cleared her throat. "Well, I'd best get this room straightened up."

"I'll help."

"Oh, there's no need. I'll come in next week and put things away and do a thorough cleaning." She glanced at him and smiled. "But thank you for the offer."

"Then will you allow me to accompany you home? I'll just ride next to your buggy. That way your family won't need to wait for you."

"That would be kind. I'd like that very much."

A ride home in the moonlight? Was that really wise? She took a deep breath. Who cared if it was wise? Jim was a perfect gentleman, and she'd be quite safe with him.

૨૦

What was he doing? Jim mentally kicked himself. He'd had every intention of watching the program then saying good night, having made the decision not to spend time with Addy until Sunday when he'd have a chance to talk to her. It wasn't fair of him to seek her out when she wasn't aware of the facts concerning his plans for the future. But one glance at the joy on her face when she saw him standing there and he could no more have left than he could have jumped in ice water.

Now as Jim held Finch back to keep pace with her buggy, his breath caught as moonlight danced in her hair and touched her brow. Inwardly he groaned. Every time he was near her, he felt the attachment grow. If something wasn't settled soon, would he be able to walk away?

Perhaps he should talk to her tonight. But no, he wanted to be able to focus his attention on her. To have a chance to read her face, in case she avoided revealing her feelings.

Anyway, a road in the moonlight wasn't the place.

The silence had gone on too long. He noticed confusion cross her face and groped for a safe conversation. "So, has Annie Bolton shown an interest in writing before?"

"Yes, she showed me a tablet full of poems and stories she's written, starting with a little poem she composed when she was seven." She smiled. "It went like this. 'The moon is smiling from the sky. If I could fly so would I.'"

Jim laughed. "Well, I've heard worse. At least it rhymes."

"Actually, I think it shows a lot of imagination for a seven year old." She smiled at him, her eyes dancing.

Oh Lord, help me. He'd found himself speaking to God a number of times lately. His recent visits to church must have had more of an effect on him than he'd realized.

"You may be right. What do you plan to do about it?"

Surprise flashed in her eyes. "Why, I'm not sure. Of course, I'll encourage her to continue her efforts and see where it leads."

He frowned and shook his head.

"What?" she asked. "What do you think I should do?"

"Maybe you could try to find a mentor to help her."

"But where? I don't know any professional writers or even writing instructors. Do you?"

"Well, no. Perhaps you could try the nearest university. They may have some suggestions." Why had he brought up the subject in the first place? What did he know about writers?

She frowned. "Maybe."

He took a deep breath. "I'm looking forward to Sunday."

Her eyes brightened. "You are? Oh, I am, too."

His breath caught. If she was this excited about their dinner together, maybe there was some hope after all.

"I'm so glad you're enjoying church services. Reverend Smith's sermons are very uplifting." She frowned. "Most of the time."

He didn't know whether to be disappointed that she was speaking of church and not dining with him or amused that she was still miffed about the sermon from Song of Solomon. Amusement won, and he pressed his lips together to keep from smiling.

She glanced his way and caught his expression. Indignation crossed her face, and he quickly composed himself.

"Yes, the reverend is quite effective. He seems to know his Bible quite well, too." Realizing that might not go over right, he added, "I especially liked his sermon about the crossing of the Red Sea a while back."

She peered at him, probably to make sure he was serious, then smiled. "Yes, it was very good even though he did get quite loud a few times."

"I'm also very much looking forward to our dinner engagement." There, hopefully she still planned to accompany him.

She nodded and gave him a sweet smile. "It was very kind of you to invite me. I'm looking forward to it as well."

They turned onto the lane leading to the Sullivan farm. Lamps in the parlor gave out an inviting warmth. A twinge of sadness bit at Jim. He hadn't experienced that since his mother died when he was twenty. His father had passed on a few years before that, but somehow his mother had managed to keep home intact until she, too, was gone.

Could he ask Addy to leave a loving family and the warmth of home to travel from city to city, state to state? Even if she agreed, would she eventually hate him for it? And what sort of life would that be for children? The situation seemed to be growing bleaker. At the moment, it seemed almost impossible.

They stopped in front of the house. He dismounted and helped her down as Jack stepped out onto the porch.

"Don't worry about the rig, Jim," Jack said. "I'll take care of it later. Lexie told me to invite you in for a late supper."

"Are you sure it won't be an inconvenience, sir?" Did they see the needy side of him? Maybe they were taking pity on him. Nonsense, they knew nothing of his parents or his lack of family.

"If I thought it would be inconvenient, I wouldn't have invited you. Come on in, Jim." He held the screen door open and motioned them inside.

Grateful, Jim grinned and started up the steps. Whatever happened Sunday, he was going to enjoy this time with Addy and her family.

fourteen

"Could you let your own child die to save others? Even if an entire town or state was in danger? Could you?"

Jim sat at attention as Reverend Smith glanced at the tiny girl sitting on Mrs. Smith's lap on the front row. "I couldn't. I wish I could say if the logs of this church building caught on fire at this moment, I would grab the first person or two I saw and help them reach safety. But I know, as sure as I'm standing here, that my first thought would be to get my wife and child away from the flames. My love and concern for all of you would not be enough for me to endanger my sweet baby girl."

What honesty! Jim stared in amazement at the courage of the man who proclaimed to his entire congregation that his love for his child would allow him to let them all die.

"But God. . ." The preacher took a handkerchief from his vest pocket and wiped his face. "God loved you and me so much that He sent His only son to suffer horribly and die for us, so that all we have to do is believe on Him and we escape the punishment we so deserve and spend eternity in Heaven with our Father."

He paused and took a deep breath. "Yes, and it's only because of that great sacrifice made by the Father and the Son that we can even call him Father. Jesus died to reconcile us to His Father and ours."

A twinge of discomfort settled in Jim's chest. Was that true? He'd always thought Jesus died because evil men killed Him and wondered why God had allowed it. But if what the preacher said was true, then He died of His own choice to pay the price for everyone's sins. But surely just believing wouldn't be enough to make up for all that agony. Would it?

His thoughts went to a small white leather Bible stowed away in a box with a few other mementos from his old life. His mother's Bible. He'd look up the verses the reverend had quoted through his sermon. He'd see for himself. And maybe he'd talk to Rafe and see what he thought.

The congregation stood and burst into song. Startled from his thoughts, Jim stood. He'd missed the last of the sermon.

As soon as the final amen was out of the preacher's mouth, Jim glanced around in search of Addy. He spotted her walking down the aisle behind her mother. She turned her head, and their eyes met. Shyness and joy seemed to battle on her face. She smiled then turned and followed her parents through the door.

Jim's heart lurched. Would she look as favorably upon him after their talk? He hoped so. But besides her parents and little sister, there was the incredibly strong bond between her and her twin sister.

He shook Reverend Smith's hand at the door then stepped into the churchyard. Addy stood talking to a group of young women. He walked over to Rafe's wagon and shook his hand, then greeted Abby, who sat with one of the twins in her lap and the other snuggling at her side. For a moment, he could almost see Addy surrounded by his children. But the vision only lasted a few seconds. As much as the two women resembled one another physically, their mannerisms and expressions were undeniably their own.

"We're going to Ma and Pa's for dinner, Jim," she said with a friendly smile. "Why don't you join us?"

"Thank you, Abby, but Addy and I are going to dinner in town." As an afterthought, he added, "You are all welcome to join us."

He didn't realize he was holding his breath until Abby burst out laughing and Rafe chuckled and said, "Don't worry, buddy. We wouldn't intrude for the world."

"Am I that obvious?" He shook his head and gave a little laugh.

"Afraid so, but we understand." He climbed into the wagon and, leaning over, gave Abby a kiss on top of the head.

Jim got the buggy and pulled up under the oak tree in the shade. He didn't have long to wait. Addy walked toward him almost immediately. He stepped down and helped her in.

"What were you and Rafe and Abby finding so funny?" she asked as they drove away.

"Oh, they were laughing at me about something." He smiled. "I made reservations at the Branson, so we'll be sure to have a nice table."

"Thank you, Jim. That was very thoughtful." She smoothed the skirt of her dress then folded her hands in her lap.

He wondered if she was thinking about her dinner there with the doctor. Jealousy seized his stomach, and he quickly got it under control. She'd sent the doctor packing. But who knew if he might not shortly receive the same fate?

There was little activity in town when they pulled up. The saloons were all closed, which helped quiet things down on Sunday. A few businessmen stood at the door of the hotel. They tipped their hats at Addy and moved aside. Families stood around talking in the luxurious lobby. The dining room doors were closed.

"I'm sorry," Jim said. "It'll be a few minutes before they open. Would you like to have a seat while we wait?"

"Addy!" A high-pitched voice sounded from across the lobby.

Jim turned to see a middle-aged woman bearing down on them. The banker's wife, Mrs. Townsend.

Addy smiled and held her hand out to the woman. "Good afternoon, Mrs. Townsend. How nice to see you."

"My dear, it's very nice to see you, too." She threw a questioning look at Jim. "And Mr. Castle. I didn't know you were acquainted with our school mistress."

Jim knew he needed to choose his words carefully. Mrs. Townsend loved to share every tidbit of news she could come by, and if it wasn't exciting enough to get the desired response, she didn't mind expanding on what she did know. It wouldn't do for her to get her hooks into Addy. "Yes, I've known Miss Sullivan's family for years. I was best man at her sister's wedding." He hoped that would be enough to curb the woman's curiosity, but from the gleam in her eye, he feared it wouldn't be. "We've just come from church and thought we'd sample the cuisine here. Perhaps you could suggest something. . ."

Before she could reply, the doors to the dining room swung open, and Jim spotted Mr. Elmer Townsend coming their way.

"A shame we have to delay our conversation, but I believe your husband is coming to fetch you, Mrs. Townsend." With a flourish he lifted her hand and leaned over just enough that his lips avoided actually touching the appendage.

With a girlish twitter, the woman took her husband's arm and pranced off to dine.

੨ঌ

Addy pressed her lips together, feeling a little faint as they walked to their table. The waiter pulled out her chair, and she sat, lifting her eyes to Jim. "Thank you. You may have saved my reputation and my job. There's no telling what she would have made of our being here together."

"You'd think that by now people would know better than to listen to her gossip." He shook his head. "But there are always those who want to think the worst and are quite willing to take part in shredding someone to pieces."

She looked at him for a moment before speaking. "Yes, but thankfully, not too many of that sort live here in Branson Town."

"Are you sure of that?" Addy gave him a quick glance,

and he added, "Of course you're right. I apologize for being cynical. Hopefully we've averted her attention from you."

She looked at the menu. The waiter brought frosted glasses of water with ice. Addy glanced at Jim. "Would you mind ordering for me? Everything sounds so delicious I can't bring myself to choose."

She studied him as he placed their order. A lock of his hair had fallen across his forehead, and Addy longed to brush it back. She blushed at the thought, averting her eyes. The waiter left and Jim leaned back.

She smiled when his eyes met hers. "You seem a little nervous today, Jim. Is something wrong?" Oh dear, she shouldn't have blurted that out. He'd think she was terribly rude.

He smiled. "You are very perceptive. I am a little nervous."

She waited for him to explain. He'd just opened his mouth when the waiter appeared with bowls of steaming soup.

She bowed her head and waited. He cleared his throat, and she opened one eye. At the look of panic on his face, she quickly closed it again.

"Dear heavenly Father," he said, "we thank You for this food from Your bounty. Amen."

She lifted her head and reached for her spoon, determined not to mention his shyness about praying.

"I'm not used to praying out loud," he said.

"Me either. Usually Pa or Rafe prays. Sometimes Ma." She dipped her spoon into the delicious smelling broth-like soup. What was it?

He smiled and took a bite of his soup. "Delicious consommé, isn't it?"

"Yes, indeed. I've never had it before." She grinned. "Or even heard of it, to be honest. But it's sort of a fancy beef broth, isn't it?"

He chuckled. "You are absolutely correct."

They continued conversing during the meal. Addy was a little disappointed he didn't share with her his reason for being nervous.

"Addy." He gave her a serious look.

"Yes?" She waited. Maybe he was going to talk about it now.

"I asked your father if I could court you."

Her heart jumped and joy filled her. "You did?"

"But I'm not sure I should have."

Her heart plunged, and her spoon slipped from her hand, falling into the soup with a splash. "Oh." She grabbed her napkin and began to blot at the tablecloth.

"I'm so sorry, Addy. That was a clumsy way to say it. Please don't misunderstand. I'd like nothing more than to court you and perhaps pursue a long-term relationship."

Pain pierced her then anger. What exactly was he trying to say? Apparently he'd changed his mind since he talked to Pa and was trying to let her down gently. He felt sorry for her. How dare he? She placed her napkin on the table and took a deep breath. "Excuse me, Mr. Castle," she said. "What gave you the idea that I might welcome your desire to court me?"

"Why, I. . ." He looked at her in surprise. "Addy, will you please let me explain?"

Apparently he wasn't fooled by her question. Well, why would he be? Hadn't she been wearing her heart on her sleeve for weeks where he was concerned? "Very well, please do explain." Her forehead felt clammy, and her throat like sandpaper.

"Addy, my job takes me all over the country. I know how much your family means to you, particularly Abby."

What was he saying? Why couldn't he work with the railroad here? Didn't he care deeply enough to do that? She opened her mouth to ask him that question, but he was still speaking.

"This job will probably end sometime in September, and I'll be moving on to another location."

But. . .why couldn't he ask the railroad to keep him here? Surely they'd have something he could do. But again, she couldn't seem to voice her thoughts.

"So you see, my dear. If we pursue a relationship, it would mean that you'd have to leave Branson." His voice caught, and he stopped.

He didn't love her. He was telling her he cared more about traveling all over the world than he did about her. If she married him, she would have to be the one to give up everything. Well, perhaps she would have been willing to travel with him if he really loved her, but it was obvious he didn't. He wouldn't even consider settling down. He'd just give her an ultimatum.

She took a deep breath and gave a little laugh. Her voice barely even trembled when she spoke. "Jim, I thought we'd already agreed to be friends. Isn't it lucky we had this talk before we went and fell in love with each other?" She stood. "Perhaps we can talk about your very interesting job another time. I really do need to be getting home."

As she walked ahead of him across the room, the pain in her heart was like a weight trying to shove her off her feet. *Oh God, please don't let him see how he's hurt me.*

fifteen

Jim pulled up beside a bluff overlooking the river and jumped out of the buggy, mentally kicking himself for making such a mess of things. He wasn't quite sure how things got so out of hand, but he really wanted to kick himself for hurting Addy. When he'd seen the pain wash over her face, he'd wanted to take her in his arms and tell her he'd do anything she desired of him, including giving up his career.

The river churned and foamed below, as if to mock him for the turmoil inside him. If there was anything he could do in this area, any type of employment he was qualified for that would support a family, he'd take it. He'd even be willing to buy a farm like Rafe's and work it, but he didn't have the slightest idea how to farm. He knew one thing. He'd do almost anything to erase the pain he'd caused her with his bad handling of the situation.

He picked up a pebble and threw it into the river, barely missing a silver-colored fish that jumped and flipped before diving back into the water.

He'd already been in Branson longer than he would have been on most jobs. But of course, the hotel, the railroad, and the lodge were interconnected as far as his job went. His analyses and the proposal for the hotel were finished. But the final analysis on the lodge couldn't begin until it was completed and they saw if business turned out as he'd projected. If so, he'd give them an extended proposal for the next three years, and his job would be over. If not, then it would be back to the drawing board.

Well, he'd start looking in Kansas City and St. Louis

before this job ran out. If he could find anything he had the skills for that paid enough, he'd take it. Maybe Addy wouldn't mind living that short distance away.

In the meantime, she'd at least expressed a willingness to be friends. Did she mean that? Or was it just a way to end the conversation?

He climbed wearily into the buggy and headed to town.

❧

For Addy, the summer days dragged on and on. She kept busy helping Ma with housework and gardening, and a couple of times a week she went over and spent some time with Aunt Kate.

Her great-aunt was following doctor's orders most of the time, but every once in a while she'd have a spell of weakness that frightened everyone but her. She'd finally told them to stop hovering over her. When it was her time to go, she'd go and be a lot better off than those who were still down here.

She seldom saw Jim, and when she did, they would speak a few polite words and be on their separate ways. Even that small amount of contact was almost more than she could bear.

Addy breathed a sigh of relief when tomatoes were ready to put up. Abby came over, and it was almost like old times, except when the thought of Jim crossed her mind.

When her family had asked why she wasn't seeing Jim anymore, she'd simply told them it hadn't worked out and left it at that. Finally they'd stopped asking. But her mother sent worried glances her way every now and then.

She might have told Abby what had happened, but her sister was overflowing with joy over the news that she and Rafe were expecting another baby around February. Addy wasn't about to spoil Abby's happiness with her own broken heart.

Once the tomatoes for the family were canned and the jars sat in double rows on the shelves at all three farms, they started hauling the remainder of the crop to the tomato factory outside Branson Town. Addy loved riding in the wagon with Ma to haul the tomatoes. Sometimes Abby and Sarah would take turns riding along while the other watched all the children.

As Labor Day approached, Addy looked forward to the town festivities, including a parade and a picnic on the river the day before school opened. She missed her students and the routine of preparing lessons and teaching. She tried to push aside the secret hope that she'd see more of Jim when she was in town every day.

After church on the day before Labor Day, she and Ma were cleaning up the kitchen after dinner. "Okay, Ma, that's the last one." She dried the serving bowl and put it away in the cupboard. "What do you want to make first?"

"Oh honey, let's get something to drink and sit out on the porch while Betty and your pa are napping." Without waiting for a reply, Ma got down two tall glasses and poured lemonade. "There's a nice breeze out today, but the house is still stuffy in spite of the open windows. We can cook for the picnic in a little while."

"All right, Ma. Here, let me take those." She took the filled glasses and followed her mother outside. They sat in matching rocking chairs, and Addy leaned back, relaxing for the first time in hours. "Oh, it does feel good out here. The breeze almost feels like autumn." If she closed her eyes she could imagine her favorite season.

"It'll be here before we know it, then winter." Ma sighed. "I hope we don't have all that ice again like last year."

"Me, too. I'd rather have a nice soft snow any day."

Ma chuckled. "Let's not ask for trouble before it's here. I'd rather sit and enjoy this wonderful September air and pretend it will last forever."

Forever. If only this moment could last forever. Or better, if time could have stood still when she and Abby were young and so happy here with Ma and Pa. Before life got complicated. Before everything changed. "I miss Abby."

Ma gave her a troubled look then took a sip of her lemonade. "I know you do, but life goes on, Addy."

"Why did God make twins to be so close when they were just going to be pulled apart when they grew up?" She could hear the self-pity in her voice but couldn't stop. Didn't really want to. "I feel sorry for Davey and Dawson. Look how inseparable they are. Just like Abby and I were. And someday that will all change."

"Change comes for everyone, not just twins. I could hardly bear it when your Uncle Will married Sarah. I'd always been big sister. Then suddenly he didn't need me."

"How did you handle it, Ma?" She'd never thought of Ma feeling that way about Uncle Will. It was strange to think of her tall, bearded, laughing uncle as her ma's little brother.

A dreamy look crossed Ma's face. "God was good. I fell in love."

"With Pa."

"That's right. I fell in love with your pa. And"—she reached over and patted Addy's arm—"I also fell in love with two sweet little rascally girls."

"I suppose we were rascals, weren't we?" She smiled at the memory.

"Well, Abby was a rascal." Ma chuckled. "You just couldn't bear to say no to her, so you went along with whatever she suggested."

"I felt responsible for her. I thought if I didn't stay close, I couldn't take care of her." Addy's heart raced. She still felt that way, only now. . .

"I know," Ma said. "Addy, your sister loves you very much, but she doesn't need you to look out for her anymore."

"I know, Ma. She has Rafe, and he would never let anything happen to her."

Ma rocked silently for a moment then said, "Your mind

knows, but I don't think your heart does. Your heart needs to believe it, too, Addy. Then you'll be able to let go and have a life of your own."

&

Jim leaned against the feed store and watched the children down by the river as they ran through the spray from the water wheel. He grinned, half wishing he could join them. The day, which had begun with a slight chill, had warmed up fast once the sun rose overhead.

He glanced a little farther down, where picnic tables had been set up. He squinted, searching for a mane of pale-gold hair among the women who were setting food on the tables.

He stood up straight. There.

On closer look, he leaned back and took his former stance against the building. It was Abby. The braids should have clued him in. He'd never seen Addy wear braids. When she put her hair up, it was always in some kind of roll or twist on the back of her head.

He was tempted to wander over in that direction to try to find her but didn't want to embarrass himself in case she snubbed him. Still, she had said they should be friends. Whether she'd meant it or not, she said it.

With determination propelling him forward, he shoved away from the building and headed down toward the picnic area. A space had been cleared for horseshoes, and he saw Rafe with a few other men lining up to take their turns.

"Hey, Jim, there's always room for one more." Rafe threw him a grin.

Jim paused and started to take a step in Rafe's direction, but a pretty blue dress with lace on the collar caught his eye. But the face above the dress wasn't the one he was looking for.

Idiot. Did you think she'd be wearing the same blue dress three years later?

"Hello, Jim."

His breath caught in his throat, and he turned at the sound of Addy's voice. He tried not to devour her with his eyes, but she was so beautiful and he'd missed her so much.

"Hello, Addy. It's good to see you." Oh, how good! If it were any better, his heart would burst through his chest.

"Hey, guess what, Jim?" Rafe grinned. "Addy learned how to fry chicken right good this summer."

"Cut it out, Rafe." Addy glared at her brother-in-law, who put his hands up in mock defense.

"How about going for a walk?" Jim said. "Some local artists have an exhibit down the street." Boring, but it was the first thing he could think of.

She smiled. "Maybe later. I need to help set the food out."

Jim watched her walk away.

"Man, you've really got a bad case of lovesick," Rafe said.

Jim glared. "Thanks for the diagnosis, Dr. Collins."

"Glad to help anytime." Rafe narrowed his eyes. "What happened with you two anyway? I thought things were going right good. I didn't want to intrude, but I've wondered."

"So did I. So did I." Jim glanced at his friend. He'd wanted to talk to Rafe about the incident with Addy before but hadn't wanted to sound like a lovelorn kid. Maybe it was time to stop hiding his feelings from his best friend. "I happened to mention the shortcomings of my job, such as leaving this place. That did it."

"You have to understand, Jim. The girls lost their real mother when they were babies, and their father was killed in a mining accident when they were eight. They sort of clung to their new family but especially to each other. They were stuck like glue." Sympathy crossed his face as he looked at Jim. "I'm afraid Addy hasn't let go yet."

Jim nodded. "I thought it might be something like that. But what do I do? I have to make a living."

Rafe shook his head. "I don't know. I sure wouldn't want to be in your place. But if she loves you, and I'm pretty sure she does, she'll come around eventually."

"Maybe. But on the other hand, that's a lot to ask of her. It's not like we'd be living a couple of farms over." And here he was again. Right back in the same place he'd started.

"Pray about it, Jim. God has the answer." Rafe headed back to the game.

Jim wandered off down the street, no longer caring about the festivities. She'd only been polite when she'd said they might be able to take a walk later. He wouldn't hold her to it, no matter how much he wanted to.

sixteen

"Sorry, Mr. Castle. Your qualifications are impressive except for one very important item. This position requires a degree in business. Perhaps you would like to place an application in our sales department." Mr. Fiferton, the head of employment services, waved a limp hand as indication the interview was over.

Jim stepped out onto the sidewalk. He'd be more than happy to work in sales, whether it meant store clerk or pounding the pavement and knocking on doors, but he knew too many salesmen who weren't earning enough to support themselves much less their families.

He stood on the sidewalk outside St. Louis's Herringdon's Department Store. This had been the last place listed in today's classifieds that sounded as though it might work.

Well, perhaps tomorrow. He hoped so. He had to be back in Branson in a couple of days to help with last-minute plans for the opening of the lodge.

Hardly a day passed that he didn't get an offer for his services, but so far he'd passed them all up in hopes that something would turn up that would be suitable. It was beginning to look less and less likely.

But he wouldn't give up. Not yet anyway. There had to be a way for him and Addy.

&

Addy pulled up in front of the school building to find Bobby waiting with a grin to take her horse and buggy to the stable. A crowd of children had already gathered in the schoolyard and were engaged in a game of hide and seek.

"Howdy, Miss Sullivan. You glad school's startin' today?"

Bobby held his hand out to help her down. Well, that was a first. The young man was growing up.

"Yes, I certainly am, Bobby. And so glad I'm done with tomatoes. I'm ready to turn that job over to someone else. I was beginning to feel like a stewed tomato."

He laughed and ducked his head. "Well, don't worry, ma'am. You sure don't look like one."

"Why, thank you, Bobby." When his face flamed, she hastened to change the subject. "Would you please check Ruby's right front hoof when you get back to the stable? I believe she may have picked up a rock or something."

"Sure thing. See you later." He waved and took off down the street toward the livery.

Shouts from the children drew her attention. She smiled and waved then stepped inside the school, removing her hat and gloves. She'd been here the week before to clean and dust and make sure the books were in order. Glancing around the room, she gave a nod of satisfaction.

She supposed it was a good thing she enjoyed teaching. It appeared she'd be doing it for a long time. Apparently she wasn't destined for matrimony and motherhood. Or even an adventurous single life. She straightened a stack of graded papers. Her dissatisfaction was probably the result of reading too many silly books growing up. She had a nice steady life and must learn to be content.

But Jim loved her, and she loved him. What if. . .

Before the thought could reach maturity, she shoved it away. If Jim really loved her, he'd ask that nice man with the railroad to keep him on here in Branson instead of sending him away. And she would never leave Abby.

She stepped outside and rang the bell more loudly than necessary in order to drive the traitorous thoughts from her mind.

She had planned some outdoor activities today, knowing the children would be restless after three months of freedom from the confines of the school.

A screech from the back of the room confirmed her decision. Carla Bright, a new student whose family had recently arrived from Kansas City, stood on top of her desk, a look of horror on her face.

Addy hurried down the aisle and looked up at the trembling girl. "Carla, what happened?"

Without turning her head, the girl pointed at Johnny. "That boy threw a mouse on me."

Whirling, Addy glared at the boy. "Johnny?"

"Aw. . .it wasn't a real mouse, Miss Sullivan. I thought she'd know. Anyone can see it's rubber." He held up the offending "mouse," which indeed was rubber and obviously so. He handed it to Abby.

She dropped it into her pocket and tapped on his desk with her ruler. "But perhaps it wasn't so clear to her that it was rubber when it came flying across the aisle and hit her. And I think you probably knew that."

He ducked his head. "Yes, ma'am," he mumbled.

Addy shook her head. "Look at me, Johnny." When he complied, she frowned slightly. "I believe you ended our last classroom session on the stool in the corner?"

He darted his eyes at the stool and back at her. "Yes, ma'am, but. . ."

"No buts. It's really a shame to have to start the year out this way, Johnny. But you must learn to think about other people's feelings. And especially a new student. I'm sure your antics didn't make Carla feel very welcome." She rested her hand on his curly top. "As soon as you can honestly say you're sorry, I'd like for you to apologize to her, Johnny. Will you do that?"

He stood and stepped over to where Carla still stood upon her desk and stared up at her. "I'm sorry. I really am. But you don't have to keep standing up there. It wasn't no real mouse." He turned and headed for the corner.

Addy glanced at the girl who still stood atop her desk. Addy was pretty sure that by now it was merely to keep everyone's attention. "Please sit down, Carla. There's nothing to be afraid of. As Johnny said, the mouse was only a toy made out of rubber." As the girl scrambled into her seat, Addy walked away but said loudly enough to be heard, "Of course, we do see a real mouse, occasionally."

When she got to the front of the room and turned around, she noticed Carla sat with a sheepish look on her face. "Well, class, I'd planned an outing this morning to the new hunting lodge. They'll be opening next week, and the owners very graciously agreed to let us tour the facility today. In fact, several mothers have volunteered to go with us and will arrive at any moment." At the outbreak of excited voices, Addy raised her hand. "But of course, we can't leave Johnny here alone, so I guess we'll have to have class instead." Disappointed murmurs arose but stopped when Addy once more raised her hand. "It's time for roll call."

Addy kept a surreptitious glance on Carla while calling roll. The girl was almost in tears. Addy was pretty sure there was more to the mouse story than had appeared on the surface. "Carla Bright," she said.

The girl raised her hand and said, "Here." She threw Addy a pained look. "Miss Sullivan, I'm so sorry. I knew the mouse wasn't real because I saw Johnny playing with it on the playground."

"I see." Addy bit her lip. "Then would you like to explain your actions?"

"I was mad because he threw it at me. I guess I just wanted to get even." She ducked her head then said, "I really am sorry. Please don't punish the class for what I did. I'll stay with Johnny."

The whole class stared. Addy wanted to take the girl, hug her, and say, "Bravo, Carla."

"Hey, I ain't no baby. I can stay here by myself."

Addy clamped her lips together to prevent a smile from popping out and glared at Johnny. "I can see you've forgotten proper English over the summer, Johnny. We'll have to work on that. But first, no more using 'ain't.'"

"Sorry."

"So, will you let me stay with him, Miss Sullivan?"

"Hmmm. Take your seat, Carla. We'll put it to a vote."

"Class, I'm going to pose three questions. After you've heard all three, I'm going to leave the decision up to you. The first option will be that we stay here today and try to reschedule our tour. The second option is that I allow Carla to stay here with Johnny. The third option is that we trust they have both learned a lesson today, we forgive them both, and we let them go with us."

As one voice, their decision roared across the classroom. But Addy made them sit and vote in an orderly way. After all, this would be a good lesson in civics.

๛

Addy's heart lurched when she saw the huge log building, looking almost the same as it had at the World's Fair. It was startling to see it standing in solitude on the bluff overlooking their own White River. What changes had been made to the inside? Would it look somewhat the same? Probably not.

She swallowed and took a look down at the two lines of children waiting to enter the building. Ten volunteer mothers were interspersed along the line to keep them in order. Addy only needed two but hadn't the heart to turn them down. This would more than likely be their only opportunity to see inside this FOR GENTLEMEN ONLY establishment.

Yes, it actually said that on the cedar wood sign beside the door. She wasn't surprised, merely a little indignant. Why, pray tell, couldn't they bring their mothers, wives, and sisters along? Maybe some of them would like to go hunting.

She gave herself a mental shake. Well, maybe their women

wouldn't want to go hunting, but there were other activities in the area they could enjoy while their husbands had their fun.

Just as she was about to lift the enormous knocker, the door swung open. Jim Castle bowed slightly as she gaped up at him. "Miss Sullivan, ladies, boys, and girls, I have the honor of being your guide today. Please step inside, and I'll show you the wonders of this historical edifice and also give you a glimpse of our plans for the future."

"Wow, look at that!" Sam's awe-filled voice rang out, almost echoing in the enormous room. "Is that a real bear?"

Jim turned and looked at the huge, brown animal that stood on its hind feet, fangs bared.

"Yes, it is, young man. Shot, stuffed, and put on display where it can't hurt a soul."

"But we don't have bears that big around here." Mrs. Allen's voice trembled. "Do we?"

"No, ma'am," Jim said quickly. "This magnificent animal was actually shot in the mountains of Wyoming."

Mrs. Allen's relieved sigh, accompanied by a few others, was audible to all.

"Perhaps we should get back to the tour, Mr. Castle," Addy suggested with a glare in his direction.

"I want to see some more bears," Sam said.

"Me, too." Johnny stared in wonder at the creature.

"Well, we'd better do as your teacher says, young fellows. But you'll see a few more stuffed animals along the way."

"You boys get back in line now." Addy shooed them with her hands. She met Jim's eyes and he smiled, an apology all over his face.

What in the world was he doing here anyway? Had he taken a job at the lodge? Did this mean he planned to stay in Branson after all? A surge of excitement rushed through her. She followed along, not hearing a word of his narration as he guided them through the building.

Jim had taken a job in Branson. He did care. But why hadn't he mentioned it to her? Had he changed his mind about wanting to court her? Pa had never said a word.

As they left the building, she gave Jim a very warm smile and offered her hand. "Thank you, Mr. Castle. It's been very interesting, and the building is perfectly wonderful."

He looked at her in surprise. "Why, thank you, Miss Sullivan. It's been my pleasure."

"Boys and girls, thank Mr. Castle for taking time to show us around and for the history lesson." Which she hoped one of the mothers could recite to her. Otherwise, how could she discuss this field trip with the students?

Among a chorus of "thank yous," the students lined up and walked down the hill to the school.

Addy's heart danced. He had decided to stay in Branson. And what other reason could there be except to please her?

seventeen

Jim wasn't sure whether to be elated or confused. The smile Addy had given him was warm and almost inviting. Wasn't it? He was more than likely imagining the whole thing. Or was it possible she'd had a change of heart and was willing to pursue a relationship even if it meant leaving her family?

He rode by the school at least half a dozen times that day. Then railing at himself for being an idiot, he took his horse to the livery stable. After that, he still managed to find errands that took him past the school at least once an hour.

Standing on the corner, Jim gazed toward the schoolyard then pulled out his watch. Almost three o'clock. He'd meet her when she came outside.

Suddenly he realized he had no idea what he intended to say to her. Was he crazy? He couldn't just come out and ask her if she'd changed her mind. He'd probably imagined she was having a change of heart. He'd better stay with his plan and continue to search for suitable employment. If and when he could come to her and offer a promising future, then the situation would be different. But until then, he was simply torturing himself.

He could see her on Sunday, perhaps, at church. That would be better than nothing. He'd been going to a church here in town for the last few weeks, and the preacher had given him a lot to think about. To the point, he'd recommitted his life to Christ. And he'd begun to look at life a lot differently. The main thing being if he and Addy were supposed to be together, God would work it out. But a sudden pang stabbed him. What if God said no? But that's what commitment to Christ was all about. Letting Him have His way in one's life. And knowing that He knows best. Perhaps he should continue with his present church for now.

Spinning around, he headed for his hotel. He had accounts to work on and needed to get on with it. Next week he'd head to Kansas City and see what was available there. It wouldn't hurt to help God out a little bit, would it?

◆

Addy searched through the cedar chest in the extra room that used to be Betty's nursery but was now used mostly for storage. Ma had sent her to find a shawl she wanted to use for a pattern. Addy's hand fell upon a soft bundle. A very soft bundle. Maybe a pillow? But it didn't feel like feathers. Should she look? But perhaps Ma wouldn't want her snooping. Still, who knew if the shawl might be inside? Guilt nibbled at her conscience. Ma had very clearly stated the shawl was folded up by itself.

Curiosity won. Addy lifted the bundle from the chest and laid it on the floor. Carefully she unwrapped the soft cotton sheet. A glimmer of red peaked out from the edge. Addy gasped. Excitement zigzagged through her as she lifted the bright red and green dresses from their protective sheet. "Ma, would you come here?"

"What is it, dear. . . ?" Ma paused in the doorway. When she saw what Addy was holding, a dreamy smile crossed her face. "Yours and Addy's Christmas dresses. I made those for you the year you came to live with me at Aunt Kate's."

"I remember." Addy swallowed past the knot that had formed in her throat. She smoothed her hand over the piney-green velvet. "I was so proud. I'd never worn anything so wonderful. I felt like a princess."

"You looked like a princess." Ma smiled. "So did Addy, even though she seldom wanted to wear dresses at all. I remember she was fussing about trying hers on, but when she saw the cherry-red velvet, she grew very quiet and didn't say another word."

"Yes, and she looked so pretty."

Ma gave her a knowing look. "So did you, sweetheart, even though you wanted the red for yourself."

Addy gasped. "How did you know that? I didn't say a word."

"No, you did not, because Abby's happiness was always first with you." For a moment a hint of sadness slid across her face. "I didn't know until I saw the look on your face that you wanted the red dress."

Addy smiled. "It's all right, Ma. I loved the green, and once we were dressed, I don't think I ever thought about it again." She laughed. "I'd never seen Abby primp before. So it was worth it."

Ma eyed the garments. "I should have used the fabric long ago, but I couldn't bear to cut into them."

"Look, Ma. The fabric is still in fine shape except for a couple of spots."

"Yes. You're right." She stooped down and placed a hand on each dress. Suddenly she stood, the dresses in her arms. "I'm going to take them in the parlor. Did you find the shawl, dear?"

"No, I'm still looking." Addy gazed after Ma. Now what was she up to? Shrugging, she began to search through the chest again. There it was. She removed the delicate shawl then closed the chest and stood up and carried it into the parlor.

Ma sat holding the dresses on her lap.

"I found the shawl, Ma. It's so beautiful."

Ma looked up from her rocker, her eyes sparkling, but ignored the shawl. "I have the most wonderful idea."

"Oh? And what is this wonderful idea? Tell me, please," Addy teased.

"Let's make Christmas suits for Davey and Dawson out of Abby's red and a dress for Betty from your green."

Addy stared at her Ma. She wanted to cut up their Christmas dresses?

Ma's eyes sparkled. "I thought I'd keep them forever, but we really need to do something with them while the fabric is still good."

"Really?"

Worry lines appeared between Ma's eyes. "Oh, of course not, dear. If you want to keep your dress, then certainly you may."

Addy closed her eyes. How silly could she get? Of course they needed to use the fabric.

"No, I think your idea is wonderful. I'll stop at the store Monday and get some white satin for bow ties for the boys and a hair ribbon for Betty."

Ma reached over and patted her. "We'll have enough from each dress to make bows for you girls to keep."

Addy's eyes swam. "Thank you, Ma. That will be perfect."

Ma's eyes danced. "Shall we tell Abby or wait and surprise her?"

Addy thought for a moment. "I think we'd better tell her. Otherwise she might take a notion to make Christmas suits herself."

"Very good idea." Ma laughed. "Let's tell her tomorrow at church."

"She'll probably want to help make them."

At least Addy hoped so. What if Abby didn't want her cherry-red Christmas dress cut apart?

❧

Addy stepped out of the church. She'd hoped Jim might come this week, although he hadn't been there since the day they'd dined at the Branson Hotel. Abby had told her he was attending a church in town and had recommitted to Christ. The news had thrilled her. But after sending him what she thought was an inviting smile at the lodge, she'd expected him to be here today.

Oh! Maybe he'd thought she was too bold. Or maybe he'd found someone else, and that was why he'd gone to work for the lodge. Although, now that she'd thought about that, she couldn't help but wonder why he hadn't just stayed with the railroad. Surely they'd have found something for him to do. Maybe he'd had to wait for an opening.

Oh, what difference did it make? Apparently he wasn't interested in her anymore. Her face flamed as she thought of her actions that day. Why she'd been positively brazen, smiling at him that way. Her thoughts continued to race until she felt like putting her hands up and squeezing her head.

"Addy!"

At the sound of her sister's voice, she looked up.

Abby stood right in front of her. "What are you day-dreaming about?" Abby laughed and grabbed her arm. "Come on. You and Betty are riding with Rafe and me. Ma invited us to dinner."

"Oh, did they leave?" She glanced around and saw the wagon pulling out of the churchyard and onto the road.

"Yes. What's the big mystery? Ma said she wanted to show me something, but she wouldn't say what."

Should she tell her? But Ma would want to be the one. She only hoped Abby wouldn't be too upset. After all, her own first reaction had been a jolt of dismay. Maybe Addy should have tried to talk Ma out of the idea. She cleared her throat. "I think I'd better let Ma tell you. You know how she is about anyone spoiling her surprises."

Abby laughed. "Yes, how well I remember. Okay, come on. Let's go so I can find out what this is all about."

They climbed into the wagon and headed toward the Sullivan farm. Some of the trees were beginning to turn, and the varying shades of green, yellow, and bronze were breathtaking. Fall had always been Addy's favorite season. Abby's, too.

"Look at the color," Abby said. "A couple more weeks and they'll really be beautiful."

Addy grinned. "You read my thoughts again, sis."

A guffaw from the back revealed that Rafe had been

listening. "I don't know how you girls can be so identical in some ways and so all-fired different in others."

"Tell me how we're different." Abby flashed a grin over her shoulder.

"Well, let's see, Tuck, my girl." Rafe held up one finger. "First, you're a whole lot meaner than your sister."

Betty giggled. "Tuck isn't mean, Rafe."

"Thank you, Betty honey," Abby said. "You tell him."

"Sure she is, Betty," said Rafe, with a grin. "And lots meaner than Addy."

Abby laughed. "Well, that's not hard. My sweet sister isn't mean at all. Tell me another one."

"I know one," said Betty. "Addy doesn't wear overalls."

Rafe howled. "I rest my case."

They pulled up to the house, laughing.

Addy inhaled deeply. If only these joyful moments could somehow be stored. If only things didn't have to change.

After dinner the men went out to look at a cow that Pa had purchased. Ma put the children down for naps while Addy and Abby cleaned the kitchen.

Afterward Addy bit her lip as she followed Ma and Abby into the parlor.

Ma patted the seat next to her on the sofa. "Come sit by me, Abby." She retrieved the bundle from a basket on the floor and removed the sheet.

Abby's eyes grew large. "Those are the first Christmas dresses you made for us, Ma."

"Yes, I've kept them all these years."

Abby grinned. "You're still sentimental, Ma. I'd have thrown them away a long time ago."

Addy stared at her twin. "You would? But Abby, you loved that dress."

"Well, sure I did. When I was eight." She laughed.

Ma smiled. "Then you won't mind if I cut your dress down and make suits for David and Dawson?"

"Oh, Ma. That's a great idea. They'll look so cute in little red velvet suits." She reached over and hugged Ma. "Can I help?"

Ma returned her hug. "Of course. Addy and I hoped you'd want to."

Abby reached over and touched the green fabric then turned to Addy. "What are we going to do with yours, sis?"

Addy smiled. "A Christmas dress for Betty. Won't she love it?"

"Oh, I'm sure she will."

"And we'll get white satin for bowties," Ma said with joy in her eyes. "And enough for a hair ribbon for Betty.

As Addy listened to Ma and Abby chattering on about the project, she shook her head. Rafe had been right. She and Abby were very different in many ways. But the sad part was that Addy hadn't realized how much her sister had changed or how little she really knew her anymore.

eighteen

Addy jumped up from her desk. Was that a gunshot?

Voices cried out and a volley of shots followed.

By now the students had jumped up and headed for the frosted windows.

"Children, sit down!" She scurried around the room, corralling students and sending them back to their seats.

"But Miss Sullivan, maybe it's outlaws!" Johnny yelled. At least he had obeyed and was seated. The older boys still stood, their excited gazes darting from her to the door.

"Don't even think about it." She headed for the window and wiped her hand across the glass, then peered out, gaping at the throng that crowded not only in front of the schoolyard but, it appeared, all over Branson Town, in spite of the bitter cold. At least the snow had held off, which was unusual for the second week in December.

A man raised his arm, his pistol pointed in the air. Addy held her breath then sighed with relief when the sheriff appeared. She couldn't tell what he was saying, but from the look on his face, he wasn't too upset.

Torn between her desire to find out what was going on and her responsibility to her students, she finally turned to the boys. "Everyone, please be seated as I instructed. There doesn't appear to be anything wrong. It seems more like a celebration of some sort."

She started as the door flew open. The sheriff's deputy stepped inside, his fur collar pulled up against the icy wind, grinning like a schoolboy.

"Ernest! What in the world is going on?"

His grin grew wider. "The sheriff saw you lookin' out

the winder. He told me to let you know everything's fine. The railroad crews have met, and the tracks are complete. The whole town is celebratin'. I gotta go." He waved at his younger brother at the back of the class and took off down the street.

The class exploded in an uproar. Addy put her hands over her ears as their shouts and whistles shattered the air, accompanied by the ones invading the room from outside. She quickly slammed the door and burst out laughing. Her students jumped up and down and swung each other around the room. She should probably put a stop to their cavorting, but why not allow them a few moments of celebration?

Finally she took a small round whistle from her desk drawer and blew three shrill blasts. The class quieted down immediately and looked in her direction.

"I know you're excited. So am I. Since it's only a half hour until lunch time, perhaps we'll cut our arithmetic lesson short and discuss this new event."

A roar of voices began to speak, and Addy blew the whistle again. "But first, I'd like for each of you to return to your seat."

One by one they dropped into their seats, breathing hard, the boys wiping their perspiring faces on their sleeves. Addy noticed a few of the girls pull out handkerchiefs and dab their foreheads. Who would guess it was so cold outside she'd had to break ice off the pump this morning?

"Charlie, would you please take my water pitcher to the pump and refill it? The rest of you get your cups out. I think you could all use a drink of water."

Heads bobbed in the affirmative.

After everyone had a few sips of water, Addy leaned against her desk and smiled.

"Maybe we'll have a new school project to talk about soon."

"Yes, ma'am," Johnny said with enthusiasm, "that play we

put on last year was a lot of fun."

"Perhaps this time we'll focus on the workers who built the tracks and the excitement of this day," Addy said.

"Building the tracks through the mountains was really dangerous," said Sally. "My pa said some men were killed."

Addy nodded. "That's right, Sally. There were a number of accidents that resulted in injuries and, in a few cases, death. The White River Route wasn't built without a heavy price."

Margaret, who'd surprised everyone by growing three inches through the summer, raised her hand.

"Yes, Margaret?"

"Now we'll finally have passenger trains coming through, and Papa said he'll take Ma and me on a train ride."

"Aw, what's so great about that?" Johnny sneered in her direction.

"That was rude, Johnny," Addy said, her voice stern. Would the boy never learn? He'd spent a number of recesses on the corner stool.

"Sorry, but I like freight trains best. They carry all kinds of great stuff."

"Perhaps Margaret would like to tell us why she wants to ride the train so badly." Addy threw the girl a smile.

Margaret's eyes lit up. "They have real dining cars with white tablecloths and real silver. And when you look out the window, you can see fields and trees and farms flying by. Or so it seems."

"Farms and trees don't fly, stupid. And neither do trains."

"Johnny. The corner." Addy glared and pointed to the stool.

"I'm sorry, Miss Sullivan. I didn't mean to say it. It just came out. Really it did."

"The corner," Addy repeated.

A twitter rolled across the room as Johnny shuffled his way across the room.

"One more sound and some of you will be joining him. It's not nice to take pleasure in someone else's discomfort."

They quieted and, one by one, raised their hands and gave their take on the completed railroad and what they thought was best about it.

After a while, Addy found herself floating in an old daydream. She stood on the top step of a train, waved to her family, and then glided down the aisle to her seat. Beaming with joy, she waved and blew kisses out the window to friends and loved ones as the train pulled away from the station. Suddenly she realized something new had been added. Always before she'd imagined she was alone. This time, in her daydream, Jim Castle stood at her side, walked by her side, and sat by her side.

She took a deep breath. Why couldn't she get the man out of her mind? She hadn't seen him since Labor Day, except for an occasional glimpse as he rode past. She'd come close to asking Abby about him a few times. Was he still working at the hunting lodge? Was he courting anyone? But she couldn't bring herself to do so.

She forced her attention back to the child who was speaking.

"My pa says Branson will get a lot more tourists now that the passenger trains can run," Alice was saying. "Especially with the State of Maine Hunting Lodge here."

"And that writer guy that wrote that book," Tommy interrupted.

Harold Wright! Of course. He and his family were camped out near the old Ross cabin. What was the name of the book he wrote? Oh yes. *The Printer of Udell's* or something like that. Rumor had it he was writing a new one. About the Ozarks. Maybe he would have some suggestions for Annie and her writing. She supposed she should obtain a copy of his book and read it before she approached him. Jim would be happy to hear she had thought of someone to help Annie.

"Tommy, it's rude to interrupt when someone is speaking," she said, "but thank you for mentioning Mr. Wright. Perhaps he'll come and speak to our class someday."

❧

Jim pushed the form through the window and paid to send the telegram. Spinning on his heel, he left the telegraph office. He'd spent the better part of November trying desperately to find suitable work in St. Louis, Kansas City, and the first two weeks of December there in Springfield. All to no avail. Now he had no choice. He'd accepted the offer from the Coney Island Park.

He'd completed his work in Branson the early part of October but kept hoping something would turn up. Most of the jobs that were suitable for him required a college degree, which he didn't have. When he'd started his own business, he'd been lucky to land that first contract that had set him up for success. He'd gotten pretty cocky. His future looked good to him. Well, he wasn't so great. Couldn't even get decent work. He'd never ask Addy to subsist on just enough to get by.

Now his options had run out. He had no choice but to get on the train the first week of January and head for New York, where he'd make a lot of money that wouldn't mean a thing to him.

He drove his rented buggy to a livery stable on the outskirts of the city, where he retrieved Finch and rode out of town. He'd carried the dream of being wed to Addy since that first day he'd met her. And after he'd gotten right with God, the feeling grew until he was certain she was the one for him. He thought they were meant to be together. But he must have been wrong. Apparently, it had merely been his own desires and not God's will at all.

All right, Lord. I give up. If You want us to be together, then work something out. If not, then okay. Thy will be done. There's nothing more I can do.

Peace washed over him, just as it had the day when he'd surrendered to God for the first time. Did surrender always feel like this? The pain of losing Addy was still there, but it was bearable. And somehow he knew they'd both be okay.

It was late when he arrived in Branson. To his surprise, people were still on the streets. He walked into the hotel and stopped. The lobby was crowded with men standing in groups, laughing and slapping each other on the back.

"Castle! This is a great day for Branson. Where've you been?" The portly man who staggered across the room had obviously been drinking for quite some time.

"Hello, Philips. I've been out of town. What's going on?" It must be big, considering the crowd.

"The tracks are complete. The White River Route is open for business. They'll be running the first passenger train next week." He hiccupped. "Lots of opportunity for us."

Jim turned away from the smell of alcohol on the man's breath. "You'd better go home, Philips, or get a room here and go to bed before you fall on your face."

A younger man came over and took Philips' arm. "Come on, Dad, the man's right. Let's get home."

"Oh, all right, son, all right. I'm coming. But I say again, it's a great day for Branson." He leaned on his tall son as they walked to the door.

Jim shook his head as he climbed the broad stairs to his room. Philips was right about it being a great day for Branson. But for Jim, it was the slamming of a door. Even though he'd had a hand in several enterprises directly affected by the railroad coming in, any happiness he felt for the town's success was snuffed out by a cold, dark hand that squeezed at his heart. He'd been so optimistic when he rode into town last spring. He'd had high hopes for his career and also for the lovely Miss Sullivan. Well, his career would be okay. But it didn't matter a lot to him now.

He kicked off his shoes and unbuttoned his shirt. The sooner he got away the better for everyone. Maybe healing would even come, eventually. He'd stay until January because he had nowhere else to be before then. And he'd accepted several invitations for the Christmas season, including the Christmas Ball.

He'd hesitated about that one because Addy was sure to be there. Although, perhaps it wouldn't hurt to get one last glimpse of her before he left. It couldn't do any more than wrench his heart out.

He wouldn't ask her to dance. Because if he did, he might not be able to leave her.

nineteen

Jim dipped the pen in the inkwell and tried again. After scribbling a few words on the sheet of paper, he wadded it and threw it into the trash basket by the hotel room desk. Leaning back into the slick leather of his chair, he drummed his fingers on the smooth cherry-wood desktop.

Writing Addy a letter probably wasn't a good idea anyway. What could he say except good-bye? Sorry it didn't work out? I love you but can't support you where you want to live? That would make her feel great.

The first rays of sun shone in the window. He'd been up all night, pacing the floor and trying to write a letter that had ended up as a trash can full of nonsense.

Better to leave things as they were. She'd probably put him out of her mind anyway. There had never been anything romantic spoken between them. Maybe a hint, but that was all. They'd been friends. He'd been an idiot to think there could be anything else.

He stood and gave the chair a kick. It rolled smoothly across the polished wood floor into the kneehole of the desk. Jim gave a short laugh. He couldn't even kick a chair over.

Striding to the door, he grabbed his hat and coat from the rack then went outside, locking the door behind him.

The lobby was empty except for a clerk behind the desk. He looked up and nodded.

Jim tipped his hat and stepped out the door onto the wood sidewalk. He stood and glanced down the street, having no idea why he'd come out in the first place. The novelty of having absolutely nothing to do was beginning to grate on his nerves.

He strode down the street, past the saloon and the new feed store. Ice stood in the horse trough out front, and gray skies promised snow. A good thing the railroad line was completed before it hit. There had been enough accidents while tunneling through the mountains and building trestle bridges over the river. A heavy snow would've shut them down completely.

He turned and walked past the other hotel. As he drew near the end of the street, he spotted Addy's buggy pulling up into the schoolyard. His heart raced. He had to admit to himself that he'd hoped to see her.

He quickened his step. Just as he approached the mercantile, Miss Martha Tyler stepped out. He tipped his hat and started to walk past the young lady. The touch of her hand on his arm stopped him in his tracks.

She tossed her head and gave him a saucy smile. "Why, Mr. Castle, you seem to be in a terrible hurry this morning." She batted her lashes and turned her green eyes fully upon his.

"Yes, I need to speak with someone." He took a step forward, but the persistent girl wouldn't turn loose of his arm.

"Will you be attending the Christmas Ball, Mr. Castle?" she asked with a simper.

"I haven't quite decided, Miss Tyler, but if I do perhaps I'll see you there?" He smiled and gently removed her hand from his sleeve. Speeding up his pace, he stepped off the sidewalk and crossed to the schoolyard, where Addy was handing the reins of her horse to Bobby.

As the boy walked away leading the horse and buggy, she turned and faced him, a strained expression on her face.

Now that they were face-to-face, he wasn't sure what to say.

She bit her lip and blinked hard as she looked at him. Were those tears?

He removed his hat. "Hello, Addy." The delicate scent of roses wafted over to him. Why did she have to smell so good? And look so wonderful?

She swallowed then ducked her head, causing the bluebirds on her hat to bob. "Hello, Jim. It's nice to see you."

"How have you been? It's been a long time." *Smart, Jim.*

"Has it?" She looked at him then averted her eyes. Why wouldn't she look at him? "Are you still working at the lodge?" she said.

"The lodge?"

"Yes, the State of Maine Hunting Lodge." She frowned. "You know. You were working there when I took the children for a tour. Right before the opening."

Why would she think. . . Oh. "I wasn't actually working at the lodge, Addy. I asked them to allow me to guide you on the tour. They did it as favor to me." He smiled.

A blush slid over her cheeks. "But I thought. . ." She shook her head and appeared confused. "Oh, never mind. How have you been?"

"Not very well as a matter of fact." He pressed his lips together, determined not to expound on his reply.

"Oh, I'm sorry." She bit her lip again and glanced toward the school. "Well, I need to get inside. The children will be here soon."

He gave a nod and moved aside so she could pass. "Will I see you at the Christmas Ball?"

"Why, yes. I plan to be there. Will you?"

"Yes, I promised Rafe and Abby. They tell me it's a grand event."

"Yes, it is. Everyone works hard to make it special. It's been held at Mr. and Mrs. Jenkins' old barn for as long as I can remember."

He nodded. "That's neighborly of them."

"Yes," she said a little too brightly. "The red bows and evergreen boughs are so beautiful, and of course there are dozens upon dozens of candles burning. And an enormous tree."

"It must be quite beautiful."

She took a deep breath. "I thought you'd have left Branson by now."

"I probably should have. I had a few things I wanted to look into first. Unfortunately, they didn't work out."

"I see. I'm sorry." She took a step toward the school. "Perhaps I'll see you at the ball, then."

"Addy, I'm leaving in January. I've accepted a job in New York." Would she care?

She stopped. For a moment she didn't move, and then she looked up at him, her face stiff. "Well, I'm sure Rafe will miss you. But after all, we did know this day was coming. I hope you'll be very happy in your new job. New York must be wonderful."

He watched silently as she walked away.

⁊⁊

Addy leaned over her desk, her head on the hard wood, and sobbed. She'd known he would leave one day. Actually, she'd expected him to be gone long before this, but she'd had no idea how badly it would hurt.

She supposed Martha Tyler was the girl he was seeing now. Addy's heart had jumped into her throat when she saw the girl lay her hand on his arm so possessively. He hadn't said anything about getting married, but it was fairly obvious. So much for her silly dreams. Martha would be the one leaving on the train with Jim Castle.

She must pull herself together before the children arrived. It was a good thing she'd gotten here early. But then, if she had arrived at her usual time, she wouldn't have run into Jim and heard the news.

Addy raised her head and blew her nose on her monogrammed handkerchief. She patted her hair back into place and stepped over to her water pitcher. Removing a cloth from the shelf below the pitcher, she put a little water on it and dabbed her face and neck.

If the children knew she'd been crying, some of them would be upset. She wouldn't spoil their day. They were excited to get the results of the essays contest. She had given them free rein over their subjects, and their essays showed a great deal about their personalities.

She went outside and found the children lined up waiting for her. Smiling, she rang the bell in case of stragglers. And sure enough, Johnny and Sam came running from around the building.

After roll call she stood in front of her desk, a stack of essays in her hand. "This is an exciting day, students. I've read and graded your papers and was quite impressed at how well you did. I've chosen the top essay for each grade level, first through eighth, which I have in my hands in no particular order except for the top two, which will be last. When I call your name, please come to the front of the class and read for us." She glanced down at the top essay on the pile, a short history on the tomato canning factory and quite good. "Cora March."

With a beaming smile, the twelve-year-old stood and walked up the aisle. Her black hair lay in two long, neat braids in front of her shoulders. She handed Cora her paper, gave the girl an encouraging nod, and then took a seat.

Cora beamed when she saw the B+ at the top. Cora read without stumbling over a word then took her seat.

"Thank you, Cora. Next, Harry Porter." The third grader jerked his head up, and his face flamed as he jumped from his seat. He stumbled through his essay, which consisted of a how-to on making a lariat, then went back to his seat, a big grin on his face.

As the morning progressed, she could tell the students were beginning to get restless. She called a short recess, and they filed out with relief on most of their faces.

Funny the difference in people. Even twins like her and Abby. Addy had always enjoyed writing essays, especially if she was allowed to choose her topic. But anyone would have thought Abby had been sentenced to slave labor. Addy had always had to help her sister with anything writing related.

She was ashamed to remember that she'd even done them for her many times. She'd suffered a lot of guilt over the cheating, crying and repenting to God, while it never occurred to Abby that it was dishonest. It was just Addy keeping her out of trouble.

It had been a vast relief to Addy when they were in eighth grade and Abby decided to write her own essay. She wrote about canoeing down the river with Rafe. Of course, the seven fish they'd caught somehow grew to twenty in the essay, but at least she wrote it herself and did a good job.

Perhaps if Addy hadn't done so many of her assignments for her, she'd have been fine a lot sooner. The thought shot through Addy's mind seemingly out of nowhere.

The children came back inside and took their seats with a shuffling of feet beneath the desks.

Addy focused on the next essay in her hand. Ah, her pride and joy. "Johnny Carroll."

"Huh?" His red mop shot up, and his mouth flew open. "Me?" He frowned at the tittering of giggles and a couple of guffaws.

"Yes, Johnny." Addy smiled at the boy. "Please come up front."

He took his paper and stared down at the A- written across the top. A look of amazement crossed his face. "Wow, I must've done real good on this paper."

"Yes, you did very well, but if you don't rephrase that sentence right now, I might be tempted to reduce your grade, young man."

"Oh, oh. I meant to say, 'I must have done very well on this here essay.'"

Addy pressed her lips against the grin that threatened to ruin her discipline. "That's better, Johnny. Please face the class and read your essay."

"Okay, first of all everyone, you need to know this ain't, I mean, isn't a real happening. I made it up. But I wish it really happened." Johnny then proceeded to read his story of a boy who went bear hunting with his father and ten brothers. He ended up saving them all. The essay was written in perfect English.

The crowning moment was when Annie Bolton came forward and read her story of a young girl growing up in England. Where she got her information, Addy couldn't imagine, but she planned to ask her after class. It was almost as if the girl had been in London herself, and Addy knew for a fact that wasn't so.

She really must contact Mr. Wright.

twenty

Jim rode Finch down the lane to Rafe's farmhouse. They'd planned to go hunting today, but sleet had begun to fall before he was halfway there. He supposed he should have turned back, but the idea of being alone with his thoughts today didn't appeal to him. He knew Rafe wouldn't mind him barging in on them. Abby either. She'd seem like a sister to him if she didn't look so much like Addy.

Rafe came out of the barn and motioned for him.

He rode Finch inside the large building and got off.

"No sense in the animal standing in the sleet when we've got this nice dry barn, now is there?"

"Thanks." He grinned. "I'm sure Finch thanks you, too."

"Might as well get that saddle and harness off him, too." Rafe shoved his hat back and grinned. "Tuck told me not to let you leave. She's making chili, and since we can't go hunting, we may as well play checkers or something, and you can eat dinner with us. Supper, too, if you've a mind. It'll probably be more of the chili."

"Can't ever get too much of Abby's chili. Guess I'll take you up on that."

After taking care of Finch, Jim helped Rafe toss hay down to the horses and mules.

By the time they left the barn, the sleet was coming down harder. "Maybe I shouldn't stay. It looks like it might get bad."

"Naw, it's just a passing storm. Won't last long." Rafe sounded pretty sure of himself, and he'd lived around here for a long time.

"Okay, if you say so." Jim chuckled and turned the brim

down on his hat as he followed his friend inside.

"Jim!" Abby stood in the kitchen doorway, wiping her hands on her apron. "I'm glad you came. You may be holed up with us for a while from the looks of the sky."

"Naw. It'll blow over," Rafe said.

She placed her hands on her hips, and her apron pulled tight across her rounded stomach. "Don't be so sure. You never can tell, Rafe Collins."

"Now Tuck, don't be picking a fight with me in front of Jim."

She grinned and placed her hand on Rafe's cheek. "Sorry. You're more than likely right anyway."

Jim averted his eyes from the casual but intimate moment. A pang shot through him. If only things could have worked out between him and Addy.

"Okay, you rascals go on in the parlor. I'll bring you some coffee in a minute." She turned to go into the kitchen.

"Hey, Tuck," Rafe said, "the coffee would sure taste good with a piece of that apple bread you made yesterday."

"Oh, all right." She tossed a laugh over her shoulder.

Jim frowned as he and Rafe went into the parlor. "Should she be waiting on us in her condition?"

Rafe grinned. "Don't let her hear you ask that. And don't worry. She knows what she can do and when to take it easy."

"I hope you know how lucky you are."

Rafe threw him a quick glance. "I do. But it's not luck. It was God who brought us together. Although, at the time, I probably thought it was my irresistible charm."

Jim laughed. "I seem to remember you had some tough times for a while, wondering if Tuck would ever see you as anything but her best pal."

Rafe quickly sobered. "Yes, that's why I know it was God. He straightened it all out for us." He grinned. "And now we're an old, settled-down married couple."

Jim nodded. "Yes, you have a great life."

"Okay, Jim. What's wrong?" He frowned. "It's that sister-in-law of mine, isn't it? She still giving you the cold shoulder?"

"I can't really blame her, Rafe. She loves her family, especially Abby. I've always heard twins have a special connection." He shook his head. "She won't leave. That's for sure. And I've about given up on finding a suitable job around here."

"Around here? You mean you'd consider giving up your business for Addy?" Rafe stared and then started setting up the checkerboard on a square table.

"Yes. I've scoured the job market in Springfield, Kansas City, and St. Louis. Anything I'm qualified for that would offer a decent income requires more education than I've had." He frowned. "I even thought of buying a farm somewhere near but realized that was stupid. I'd be broke the first six months. What do I know about farming?"

Rafe shook his head. "You'd also be miserable doing something you're not cut out for. I knew you were crazy about Addy, but I didn't know it was that bad. I don't know if I'd have even gone that far for Tuck." He paused. "Yes, I would've done anything for Tuck."

"I'm thinking about pulling out earlier than I'd planned. I don't know if I can handle seeing her at the dance in someone else's arms."

Abby came through the door. She carried a tray laden with coffee mugs and a plate of apple bread.

Her face looked frozen. Had she heard what he'd said? She put the tray on a small table and turned to look at Jim. "Does Addy know you've been trying to find work so you won't have to leave?"

"Tuck, were you listening at the door?" Rafe threw a frown in her direction.

"Not till I heard my sister's name," Abby shot back then turned to Jim again. "Well, does she?"

"I don't know how she would. I've never mentioned it to her. But I spoke to her a few days ago. Somehow, she had gotten the idea I worked at the hunting lodge."

"Oh." She frowned again then planted her hands on her hips. "You and Addy are pathetic. You love each other. There is a way to work this out. Don't you dare leave until after the ball. Give God a chance here."

Rafe frowned. "God or Tuck?"

"God, of course. Often on this earth He uses people, though." She turned and left the room.

Jim stared after her, dumfounded. What just happened here? She seemed pretty sure Addy loved him. He looked at Rafe in confusion.

Rafe laughed. "That's my girl. I'd listen to her if I were you, my friend. She knows her sister pretty well. And you never know what can happen when my Tuck gets on the trail."

❧

Mrs. Bright passed out decorated sugar cookies, homemade coconut bonbons, and cinnamon apple cider then clapped her hands together. "Eugene," she scolded, "put that cookie down. We haven't thanked the good Lord for it yet."

Addy grinned as the boy dropped his cookie like a hot poker and folded his hands.

A tree stood in the corner of the room, nearly touching the ceiling. She and the children had made ornaments earlier in the week, and yesterday they'd decorated. Mr. Carroll had put the homemade angel on the tree's top for them when he'd come to pick Johnny up after school. The floor beneath the tree was covered with brightly wrapped gifts.

Mrs. Carroll sat at the organ and played Christmas carols. Addy was thankful she had volunteers today. A mix of sleet and snow had been falling since noon. She hadn't been sure they'd show up. But out of the six scheduled, Mrs. Bright and Mrs. Carroll had arrived with smiles on their faces and baskets of goodies to add to the ones Ma had sent.

As the children bit into the sweet confections, Addy attempted to keep a smile on her face, even though the scene she'd witnessed in front of the mercantile a few days earlier played over and over in her mind. It had been, ever since she'd seen the intimate moment between Jim and Martha.

She jerked her thoughts back to the classroom and her excited students. They would have the gift exchange in a few moments, and then Addy would pass out Ma's little treat bags before the children were dismissed for the Christmas holidays.

Ma had made brightly colored flannel bags and filled each with an apple, a handful of walnuts, ribbon candy, and a candy cane. The walnuts and apples were from their own cellar. Ma had purchased the ribbon candy from Mr. Hawkins' store, which she still preferred over the new mercantile, but the candy canes she'd made herself.

Johnny's shrill voice rang out in the last note of "Jingle Bells."

Addy clapped her hands. "All right, boys and girls. We're going to take a short break for whoever needs one. Please come back inside after you've been to the outhouse. The snow is getting harder. When we return, it will be time for the gift exchange."

They all scampered outside, several making a beeline for the outhouse, while a few began scooping up snow for a snowball fight.

"They're sure having fun, aren't they?" Mrs. Bright said, her eyes shining as she watched through the window.

"Yes, and I can't bring myself to scold them," Addy said. "This is the first real snow of the season."

Mrs. Carroll hurried to the window and peered out. "Oh, dear. Do you think we should go ahead and dismiss the children?"

"No, some of the parents will be here at two to pick their children up. If it gets too bad, Mr. Travis at the livery stable will hitch up a wagon and take the rest of them home." Addy was grateful for the kindly old man who'd volunteered his services a couple of years ago. So far, he'd only had to do it once, but Addy knew she could count on him.

When the children were back inside and their wraps drying near the stove, she smiled at them. "Who would like to help me give out the gifts?"

Annie's hand went up first. The girl took turns pulling out boys' and girls' gifts. She handed them to the ladies who passed them out.

"Aww. The snow's stopped." Sam's disappointment rang across the room.

Addy glanced at the window. Sure enough, only a few flakes fell, and the sky seemed to be lighter than before.

"Don't worry, young man," Mrs. Carroll said. "Before long you'll be complaining because there's so much snow you can't go out and play."

A smile tipped Addy's lips. That was so true. Early snow was fun, but around February, the winter could seem dark and long.

The children tore into their gifts, and soon the sounds of pleasure and "thank yous" were heard. Then the paper and ribbons were wrapped up to take home or throw away, depending on their condition. The smaller children squealed with delight when Addy passed out the bright-colored treat bags. And even the older children had grins on their faces.

The parents of the children who lived outside of town arrived promptly. Those students who lived in town yelled quick good-byes to their friends and took off toward their homes.

Mr. Carroll came inside and banked the fire while Addy and her two volunteers straightened up the room.

"Now, honey, will you be okay to drive home alone?" Mrs. Carroll stood in the doorway and darted a fearful look at the sky.

"Please don't worry about me, Mrs. Carroll," Addy said. "I don't have that far to drive, and there's not too much snow on the ground."

"But what if it starts up again?" She wrung her hands.

"Now, Polly. She'll be all right. Even if the snow does start, she'd be home before things got dangerous."

"Well, if you're sure." She patted Addy on the shoulder. "But you hurry up and get home, now."

"I will, Mrs. Bright. I'll be on my way in five minutes."

As Addy drove home, she forced her mind away from thoughts about Jim. After all, Abby was coming tomorrow to help Addy and Ma cut and sew the boys' little suits and Betty's Christmas dress. It would be a wonderful day.

She urged her horse forward, and the buggy picked up speed. She had her wonderful family and a community full of old friends. Who needed Jim Castle anyway? She'd been happy before he came into her life, and she'd be happy again.

Then why did she feel so torn inside? As though something had been ripped from her. Something that belonged.

twenty-one

"Brrrr." Addy rubbed her hands together as she stepped inside after looking down the lane for Abby's buggy. "I'm glad I don't have to go anywhere today."

"No sign of Abby yet?" Ma sat by the fireplace in her rocker. She and Addy had measured Betty for her Christmas dress the night before and cut the green velvet fabric, but they were waiting for Abby to bring her patterns for the boys' outfits.

"No, but I'm sure she'll be here any moment. She knows we need to get started." Addy hoped having her sister there all day would distract her from the disturbing thoughts of Jim that continuously ran through her head.

At the sound of horses and wagon wheels, she jumped up and ran to the door. Grabbing her shawl, she slipped out and shut the door behind her to keep out the cold. The wagon bumped up and down behind the running horses, snow flying beneath wheels and hooves. Her sister yanked on the reins at the barn doors.

"Land sakes, Abby," Addy yelled across the yard, her hands on her hips. "What are you trying to do? Have the baby before Christmas?"

Abby laughed. "I'll be in as soon as I take care of the horses."

Addy took off across the yard, reaching her sister just as she slid off the wagon seat. Addy grabbed the reins before her sister could and led the rig into the barn, handing the horses off to Pa.

Clutching her shawl tightly around her shoulders, Addy stormed out of the barn. "Abby, you need to start being more careful."

"Oh sis, I'm fine, but you're going to freeze, running out here without your coat." But she took the steps to the porch slowly.

Addy put her arm around Abby and opened the door. "Come on inside and sit down."

"Hi, Ma," Abby almost sang as she stepped into the parlor. "Am I late?"

"Not at all, dear." She lifted her cheek for her daughter's kiss and smiled. "You did remember to bring the patterns, didn't you?"

"Yes, ma'am." She slipped them from her coat pocket. "I'll lay them on the kitchen table for now."

"Tuck!" Betty ran in and grabbed Abby around the legs. "You're here."

"I sure am, little Betsy Boo." Abby patted the three-year-old on the head."

"Betty, you mustn't grab Abby around her legs like that." Ma frowned. "You might trip her and cause her to fall."

"I'm okay, Ma." Abby reached down and gave Ma a kiss. "Is that coffee I smell?"

Without waiting for an answer, she headed for the kitchen with Betty trailing behind.

Addy followed. "I'll help. Ma, do you want tea or coffee?" she called back over her shoulder.

"Neither, dear." Ma's voice trailed after them. "If you girls need help cutting the suits out, call me. I want to start basting the top of Betty's dress to the skirt."

Addy poured coffee for her and Abby while her sister laid the fabric out on the table. Last week Addy and Ma had carefully removed the stitches from the dresses and removed the sleeves and collars. Now she helped her sister pin a pattern to the soft velvet.

Betty rubbed her hand over the fabric. "Pretty."

"Yes, it is pretty, sweetie. But you mustn't touch now. Soon it will be full of sharp pins."

"Okay." She perched on a stool behind the table.

"I never used to like sewing," Abby said. "But I just love making things for my little sugars."

Addy glanced at her twin, and a pang of envy shot through her. Quickly she pushed it away. She was happy for Abby, and even if she should never marry and have children of her own, she would not allow jealousy to raise its ugly head and come between her and her beloved sister. "Who wouldn't love sewing for those two little darlings?" she said around the pins in her mouth.

"Be careful, silly. You might swallow one of those things." Abby frowned. "Use the pin cushion."

Addy removed the pins from her mouth and stuck them in one of the pincushions scattered around the table. "When did you get so bossy?" she asked.

Abby grinned. "When I got married. You weren't around to boss me, so I decided to try being the boss. Rafe didn't take to it though."

"So I guess you'll have to settle for bossing Davey and Dawson."

Abby shrugged. "Half the time they try to boss me. But I'm attempting to put a stop to that."

Betty giggled. "Davey and Dawson don't boss you."

"No, but they would if I let them." Abby flashed a grin at Betty.

They finished pinning and cutting the tiny trousers.

"I hope Rafe won't think these look sissified," Abby said, cocking her head with a frown.

Addy laughed. "Sissified? They're just babies."

"I know. I was teasing. But he'll have them in boots before you know it. Just you wait and see." Abby picked up her coffee mug and took a drink. "Cold already." She poured it back in the pot and moved it to the hot part of the stove.

"We probably need more wood in there," Addy said. "We'll need to start cooking pretty soon. It's eleven o'clock."

"Pa'll be hungry as a bear after splitting wood all morning. I'd have helped if he'd have let me."

"Oh, you were going to split wood in your condition," Addy said. "That would have been a sight to behold." She picked up one end of the fabric, being careful of the pins.

"I thought Pa was hiring someone to help out around here," Abby said, picking up the other end and helping Addy carry it into Addy's bedroom.

"Everyone's been so busy on their own farms, he hasn't been able to find anyone."

"I'll tell Rafe to ask around. Pa isn't getting any younger."

Addy laughed. "He's not that old, silly. He can outwork a lot of younger men."

"I know. Still, it wouldn't hurt for him to slow down a little."

Ma came into the kitchen and started preparing the noon meal. Soon the aroma of pork chops filled the entire house.

After lunch, Pa went back to splitting wood, and Ma put Betty down for a nap.

After Addy and Abby had cleaned the kitchen, Addy said, "We'd better get the fabric and take it into the parlor. We have a lot of sewing to do."

"Wait a minute, sis. Let's step out on the porch where we can have some privacy. I need to talk to you about something."

"What is it? We need to get busy or we won't get done."

"We don't have to finish today." Abby said. "I can work on finishing up the boys' suits in my spare time. This is important. It's about Jim."

On wooden feet, Addy followed her sister to the front porch. They'd grabbed their coats, but Addy still shivered. She stared at Abby. "If you're going to tell me he's leaving town, I already know."

"I know you do. But did you know he's been riding all over Missouri for weeks trying to find work so that he won't have to leave you?"

Addy gasped. "What? What do you mean?"

"Just what I said. Jim knows you won't leave home, and he loves you so much he's searched high and low for a job, but nothing turned up that paid enough to take care of a family. He even considered buying a farm, but the man can't even milk a cow. He'd be broke before a year was out."

Jim loved her? That much? Confusion beat at her mind. But why didn't he stay here in Branson and work for the Missouri Pacific?

"But. . .Abby, why doesn't he talk to his boss about staying here and working for the railroad? Surely they have something he can do in this area."

"What? Jim doesn't work for the railroad, you silly thing. He has his own business."

Addy laughed. A sick sounding little half sob that wasn't a laugh at all. "Of course he works for the railroad. He has business meetings with them all the time."

Abby shook her head. "That's what I thought, too. But it's not so. He's some kind of consultant, and he helps people get their businesses in shape so they make more money or something. He's been on a job, which included the White River Line and the Branson hotel and some other businesses. They pay him to do this, and when the job is over he goes somewhere else."

"But why didn't he tell me?"

Addy's hand pressed her shoulder. "I guess he thought you knew."

"Then he was going to give up his business for me?"

Abby shrugged. "Looks that way. Rafe told me Jim has turned down at least four or five offers since his job here ended in September. But he can't wait any longer. And he's about sick from having to leave you."

Addy closed her eyes against the tears that filled them. "Oh, Abby," she whispered. "What have I done?"

"The important thing is what are you going to do?"

"But what can I do? He's going to New York."

"Go with him. You love him, don't you?"

"Yes," she said. "But you're telling me to leave you, Abby."

Abby groaned. "Addy, you've been taking care of me all your life. Now it's time to get one of your own."

"But. . ."

"Listen, sis, I love you, and I know you love me, but you don't need to take care of me. I have Rafe. And more important, I have God." She stopped and bit her lip. "I don't mean to sound mean, sis, but if Rafe were going to New York, I'd leave you in a minute."

"I never thought we'd be apart," Addy said. "Ever since Ma died, then Pa's accident, I felt like I needed to watch over you."

"I know. And I thought we'd both get married and live right next to each other and raise our babies together."

A cold, hard fist seemed to shove itself into Addy's heart. "I don't know if I can do it."

Abby took her hand. "The train comes right into Branson now. It's not like we can't visit each other."

"That's true." A little glimmer of hope sparked in Addy. "Do you think Jim still wants me to go with him?"

Abby laughed. "I wish you could have heard him. Of course, if he'd known I was listening, he'd never have opened up to Rafe the way he did. Aren't you glad I snooped?"

How could she have been so stupid? She'd thought he was putting his job before her when all the time he was willing to sacrifice a career he loved for her. "I don't know what to do."

"You'll see him at the ball Friday night. Talk to him," Addy said.

Horror stemming from humiliation washed over her. "I can't just go up to him and say, 'I changed my mind. Take me with you.'"

Abby laughed. "I would, if it were Rafe."

"I think your memory is a little faulty," Addy said. "You thought Rafe wanted to marry Carrie Sue, and you almost had a conniption fit trying to decide what to do."

"Hmm. I guess you're right. I'd forgotten about that." Abby thought for a minute. "I guess you should just go and leave things in God's hands."

Now why hadn't she thought of that?

twenty-two

Nostalgia engulfed Addy as she sat on her bed and sorted through a box of mementos. She took a deep breath and let it out with a ragged *whoosh*. Matching gold wands represented the fifth grade school play when she and Abby had played identical fairies. A sound halfway between a sob and a laugh erupted from her throat. She'd had to practically drag her sister to school that night.

"Addy, you haven't even started dressing for the ball." Ma stood in the doorway. Her deep-blue dress deepened her eyes until they appeared almost as if one were gazing into a midnight sky. Her black hair, with only a few white strands at her temples, was arranged softly around her face with the back pulled up in a smooth chignon.

"You're so beautiful, Ma." Addy whispered the words. No wonder Pa was still so much in love with her. Not that looks were everything. Ma was a wonderful woman, too. But Addy hadn't realized just how physically beautiful Ma was until this moment.

"Oh, you just think that because I'm your mother." She smiled. "Come now. Get dressed or we'll be late. I want to get your pa on the dance floor as early as possible so that he can't use tiredness as an excuse."

Addy rose. "What should I do about Jim?" She'd shared with her mother what Abby had told her about him. But Ma hadn't yet offered any advice.

Ma brushed a lock of hair back from Addy's face. "No one can tell you what to do. That's your decision."

"But what do you think I should do?"

"Are you in love with him?" Ma leaned back and looked

closely at her face.

"Yes. I love him so much I've been in agony for months."

"Well, there is your answer. Of course you must let him know that you're willing to go with him."

How could Ma speak so emphatically? Like that was the only answer. What about leaving family? What about her job?

"But Ma, I'll be far away from here most of the time. Jim travels all over the country. Even to foreign lands sometimes." At the words, her heart raced, and a jolt of excitement ran through her.

Ma smiled. "You have a love of adventure in you, Addy. I've always known that."

Addy sobered. "Ma, if I go, I'll be so lonely without you."

"Probably. In the beginning. But God will replace the loneliness with a brand-new life. And brand-new people. A husband. Children. New friends."

"How can you be so wise, Ma? You've hardly been out of Missouri."

Ma's eyes sparkled. "I always wished I could go downriver on the *Julia Dawn*."

"You did? Really?"

"I really did. And as happy as I was when your dad sold his boat and took up farming, I'd have gone to the ends of the earth with him, if he'd asked."

"Oh, Ma. What about Abby? How can I leave her?" She picked up the box she'd been going through. "Look. Every memory I have includes Abby. Sometimes it's like we're one person."

Little furrows appeared between Ma's eyes. "You are a whole person, Addy. You don't need your sister to make you whole. Only God can do that. And as for your memories, we all have them, sweetheart. Some good and some bad. But in order to follow God's will for our lives, we must be willing to leave some things behind."

"I know. I know Jesus said that many times. But how do I know God wants me to go with Jim?" This was a question she'd asked herself for days. She knew it needed to be settled in her heart before she could make a decision.

"God isn't deliberately keeping you in the dark about His will for you," Ma said. "The Bible says, 'If any of you lack wisdom, let him ask of God, that giveth to all men liberally, and upbraideth not; and it shall be given him.'"

As Ma spoke the familiar scripture verse, peace washed over Addy. "Thank you, Ma."

"You are welcome, daughter," Ma said with a smile. "And now, I think you had better get ready. You know we have to drop Betty off at Rafe's parents' house on the way."

≥•

Jim leaned against the wall inside the Hawkins' old barn. Red bows decorated fresh green boughs, and the pine and cedar gave a festive look as well as aroma.

Jim scarcely noticed any of it. His eyes were on the wide, festooned double doors.

Rafe and Abby had arrived a few minutes ago, decked out in finery. He'd started at the first sight of Abby. Dressed in a green satin gown, with her hair all fancied up, for a moment, he'd thought she was Addy, and his heart had almost stood still. Then she'd turned, and the oversized shawl couldn't hide her growing stomach. Plus the movement and the expression on her face were all Abby. They'd said hello in passing and headed for the refreshment table.

The Packard brothers were tuning up their guitars, so Jim assumed the dancing would start any moment.

"Hey, Jim," Rafe said, coming to stand by him. "I need to talk to you before Addy gets here."

Coldness ran over Jim. What now? More bad news? Had she met someone?

"I thought you should know that Addy thought all this time you worked for the Missouri Pacific."

"What?"

"Tuck told her how you'd been job hunting because you didn't want to leave her, and she wanted to know why you didn't just keep a railroad job here in Branson." Rafe grinned. "She asked why you needed to hunt for a job when you were already working for the railroad and all you needed to do was ask them to assign you to Branson. Or something like that. Anyway, Tuck told her about your business, and now she's feeling bad about the way she treated you."

"Are you sure about this?"

"Yes, she's still pretty squirrely about not wanting to leave her family, especially Tuck. But she's softening some." He slapped Jim on the back. "Just thought you should know."

"Thanks, I appreciate it."

Rafe turned away, and just then, Jack and Lexie walked through the doors.

Jim stood straight, his eyes glued on the entrance. He took a sharp breath as Addy stepped inside. Moonlight streamed in, bathing her in its glow. Her pale-blond hair cascaded in loose curls down the back of her deep-scarlet gown. A gold locket rested on her throat.

She turned, and her eyes met his. They widened and shock filled them. As though in a daze, she turned and followed her parents across to the refreshment table.

❧

Shock hit Addy as her eyes rested on Jim. As though through a tunnel, his voice resounded in her head, telling her he'd loved her from the moment he saw her. As though looking through a kaleidoscope, she saw his tenderness toward her and the revelation that he loved her enough to give up a career he'd worked and fought for. Indescribable happiness pierced through her. Her legs trembled.

What had she been thinking? Of course God had brought Jim into her life. This was a strong man. If not for God and the love He'd put in Jim's heart for her, he'd have swept her out of his mind months ago. Joy swelled up in her, and she knew she needed to find a chair before she ended up on the floor.

Addy accepted a cup of punch from Carrie Sue's little sister and went to one of the tables. As soon as she was seated, she turned slightly and met his watching gaze. She averted her eyes and pressed her lips together but couldn't keep them from tilting upward at the corners.

Horace Packard stepped up to the raised platform at the back of the room. "Ladies and gentlemen, everyone line up for a lively, toe-tapping Virginia reel."

Among laughter and catcalls, couples, young and old, formed two lines. Addy groaned as she saw Dr. Fields head her way from the front of the barn. Just before he arrived, a tall shadow crossed her vision, and she looked up to see Jim bow.

"May I have this dance, Miss Sullivan?" His smile was uncertain as though he half expected her to refuse.

"I'd be delighted, Mr. Castle." She placed her hand in his and stood.

The next few moments of toe-tapping fun flew by with no chance to speak.

The dance ended, and the couples all reunited, some waiting for the next dance, others falling into their chairs.

"Addy."

"Jim."

Before either could continue, a sweet, sweet sound started low and muted and then grew, almost heart-wrenching in its intensity. Startled, Addy looked toward the platform. Abby sat, her bow held high. Their eyes met for a moment. Then Addy closed her eyes and let the haunting notes of Abby's violin caress her soul.

As the sweet strains of a waltz filled the room and Jim took her in his arms, the thought crossed Addy's mind that her sister must really want to get rid of her. She smiled to herself and relaxed in Jim's arms.

"You are so beautiful tonight, you take my breath away." Jim's voice was soft on her ears, his words tender to her heart.

"Thank you," she said, her voice trembling.

Weakness washed over her, and she prayed he wouldn't let go because she'd surely land right on the floor. But in spite of the weakness, a peace she'd never known washed over her.

Oh God, thank You for straightening out my thinking. Abby never really needed me. I was the one who needed to be needed.

The music came to an end. Jim asked, "Would you care to go outside for some air? It's quite stuffy in here."

They walked across the room, and Abby grinned at them as they walked by. On the way out, they stopped to get cups of hot cider. They strolled across to the fence and leaned against it.

Addy shivered, and Jim reached over and adjusted the shawl she'd thrown around her shoulders.

"Why didn't you wear a coat?" he said.

She laughed. "You sound like my sister. She said the same thing to me a few days ago."

"Your sister is very wise." He smiled, and the crinkling of his eyes made her knees go weak again.

"Yes, she certainly is, but as a matter of fact, my coat is in our buggy. And must we talk about my sister?" Oh no. Had she actually voiced that thought?

He laughed. "As a matter of fact, I do have some things I'd like to talk over with you. I was going to ask if I could take you for a drive tomorrow."

"Yes, I'd like that." She looked up at the night sky. "Of course, it looks as though we might have snow."

"Snow won't keep me away," he said. "What I have to say is much too important."

A gust of icy wind hit them suddenly, and Addy shivered again.

"Let me get your coat."

"Thank you, but we should probably go inside."

Disappointment clouded his eyes, but he nodded. "Of course."

She laid her hand on his proffered arm, and they went inside.

Within a few moments, the wind had increased and roared against the barn, shaking the sturdy walls and roaring down the chimneys.

The guests hurried to get their things together.

Ma appeared at her side. "Dear, we need to go home now. Pa thinks a storm is coming. Abigail and Rafe are going to take Betty home with them, or if the wind gets worse they'll all spend the night with Rafe's folks." She nodded at Jim. "Good night, Mr. Castle. Please be careful on your way back to town."

Jim walked Addy to the wagon. She turned and watched as he saddled Finch and rode away.

twenty-three

Addy wiped the frost off the parlor window and peered out at the deep drifts piled high against the house and outbuildings. Would he show up? He'd said snow wouldn't stop him, but surely he hadn't realized how much would fall in the night. The only way he'd get through this was by horse or sleigh. When the snow stopped earlier this morning, Rafe had brought a bundled-up Betty home in his sleigh.

She was almost beside herself with nerves. Now that she'd come to her senses, what if he didn't ask her to marry him and leave Branson with him? After all, he couldn't know that all she wanted now was to be with him, even if he took her to the other side of the world. Would she dare bring up the subject?

"I hear sleigh bells." Betty ran to the window and looked out.

"Are you sure, Bets? I don't hear them." Addy squinted and peered again through the frosty pane.

"Yes, I'm sure." Betty said. "Maybe your ears don't work as good as mine."

"Maybe they don't work as well as yours, sweetheart."

Betty hunched her shoulders and grinned. "That's what I said, silly."

Wait, maybe Betty was right. Addy ran to the door and flung it open. She heard the jingling of bells just before the single-horse sleigh came around the bend of the lane. Quickly she shut the door before Jim could see her. After all, it wouldn't do to appear too eager.

Betty gave an impatient little stomp. "Why'd you close the door, sister? He's almost here."

164

"Well. . .umm. . .I didn't want to let cold air in."

"Oh." She wrinkled her brow and gave Addy a suspicious stare.

At the knock on the door, Betty flung it open. "Hi, Mr. Jim."

"Well hello, Miss Betty," Jim said with a bow. "It's mighty cold out here. Is it all right if I come in?"

Addy blushed. "Please come in, of course. May I take your hat?"

"I'd better take care of it myself. I dropped it in a snow bank a few minutes ago, and it's wet." He hung it on the hat rack.

Pa stepped out into the hall. "Come in and sit by the fire, Jim. I think Lexie just took cinnamon rolls out of the stove."

"Thank you, sir, but if you don't mind, I'll wait until Addy and I get back from our ride." He gave her a questioning look. "That is if you'd still like to go. I have a pile of warm blankets for you."

"Yes, a sleigh ride will be fun. Let me get my coat and gloves."

"And a hat," Betty piped up. "Don't forget your hat, Addy."

"Oh, thanks, Bets, but will a wool scarf do?" She smiled and gave her sister a kiss on the cheek before she and Jim walked to the sleigh.

He helped her in then tucked blankets around her before getting in himself.

The sleigh glided smoothly across the snow, and Addy leaned back against the seat in satisfaction. "Are we going any place in particular?" she asked.

"I thought we'd go down by the river or maybe over to the churchyard so we can sit and talk," he said. "Unless there's someplace else you'd like to go."

"No, that would be fine." She licked her lips, suddenly nervous again.

Snow began to fall in soft white flakes as they pulled into the churchyard.

"Oh, dear." Addy pulled her collar closer around her neck. "I hope it doesn't get any harder."

"I can take you back home if you'd like. I suppose we can talk another time." The disappointment in Jim's voice would have made up her mind, if she'd needed it.

"No, that won't be necessary. It's not snowing that hard. And look how beautiful it is." Addy took a deep breath as she glanced around. Snow draped the trees that surrounded the church and yard, and drifts billowed up against the weathered logs.

"It almost looks like a picture, doesn't it?" she said.

"Yes, it does. I feel like singing 'Jingle Bells.'" He grinned.

She giggled. "Me, too."

He reached over and wiped snow off the red wool scarf she'd placed over her hair. Then he paused and looked deeply into her eyes. Her breath caught, and she lowered her lashes.

"Addy, look at me." He lifted her chin. "I love you. That was the first thing I wanted to say."

She couldn't escape the happy sigh that escaped. He loved her. Her heart beat rapidly. Could she say it? Should she? Casting caution aside, she whispered, "I love you, too."

Joy slid over his face, but immediately he sobered. "I tried to find work, so we could be together without your leaving the home and family you love."

"I know. Abby told me." She raised her eyes and met his. "Jim, I didn't understand. I've been behaving like a child hoping everything would work out the way I wanted it. But life doesn't always work out the way we have it planned."

"Does that mean. . . ?"

"It means I've realized sometimes God's plan is different than ours, but His is always the right one." She trembled as she allowed her love for him to shine from her eyes. "I want to go wherever you go. If you still want me."

"Still want you? Oh my darling girl. . ." he said. "And we can visit often now that the railroad is complete. Who knows? Now that those Wright brothers have had a successful flight, we might even fly here someday."

Addy giggled at the ridiculous remark. "I think I'd rather stick to the train."

She gasped as snow began to come down heavily. "Jim, this isn't light snow anymore."

"You're right. I need to get you home. But first, I have a very important question to ask, and I don't want to wait any longer. Addy, will you please marry me?"

"Yes," she whispered, "I will."

As a curtain of snow fell, Jim bent his head and kissed her waiting lips.

⁕

Addy stood on the top step of the train and waved, feeling the comfort of Jim's chest behind her.

Ma wiped the corner of her eye with her handkerchief but managed to throw a tremulous smile Addy's way.

Little Betty clung to her mother, sniveling and waving. " 'Bye, Addy," she said for about the umpteenth time. "Don't forget to write me a letter."

"I won't forget, Bets. I promise. Good-bye." Addy's voice cracked, and tears rushed up, threatening to overflow. She averted her eyes from her little sister just for a moment, then forced a big smile and turned her gaze back on her family.

Pa appeared stern, but Addy knew he was fighting back tears. Funny how men thought they had to be so brave. He cleared his throat. "Take care of my little girl, Jim."

"I will, sir. I promise." Jim's voice was deep with emotion.

Rafe and Abby stood to one side. Worry rose up in Addy as she looked at her sister. Abby stood stock still, a smile frozen on her face. Grief filled her eyes.

Addy touched her hand to her lips and blew her a kiss.

Jim pressed gently on her waist. "We need to find our seats, sweetheart."

Addy waved again then walked down the narrow aisle

at her husband's side. She scooted into her seat next to the window while Jim put her hatbox in the space above. Waving to her family, she examined each face.

The train lurched and began to roll slowly forward.

Addy hung on to the arm of her seat and continued to wave.

Suddenly Abby broke loose from Rafe's protective arm and took a step after the train. "Addy! Good-bye. I love you so much!" She continued to wave as the train crept slowly forward.

"I love you, too, Abby. I love you, too. Don't worry, we'll visit!" She blew another kiss.

"I know. I. . ." The rest of her sentence was drowned out as the train whistled loudly and the wheels picked up speed. Abby grinned and blew a kiss back then buried her face in Rafe's shoulder. The train picked up more speed, and Abby leaned back against Rafe.

Addy put her hand to her throat. Her sister would be all right. She had her husband, and they both had God. Peace flowed through her as she turned around. She looked at Jim and met love in his eyes.

"I love you, Mrs. Castle," he said.

Suddenly amazement washed over her. It was just like her dream, from the moment she stood on the train step then walked with her husband up the aisle and sat beside him as the train left Branson. "I love you, too, Jim Castle."

A ripple of delighted laughter escaped her throat. Life would be one grand adventure with her handsome, dashing Jim. And she didn't need to worry about leaving home. She'd heard the phrase "Home is where the heart is." And her heart was right here where it belonged.

Jim eyes crinkled as he smiled down at her. A lock of almost-black hair fell across his forehead as he bent and kissed her tenderly on the cheek.

epilogue

Addy stepped through the gate, holding onto Jim's arm, then stopped and stood still. Closing her eyes, she inhaled deeply. The smell of wood smoke tantalized her senses, taking her back in time to the Sullivan farm and Ma's old wood stove. She could even smell chicken frying.

Her eyes flew open, and she glanced up at her husband. "It smells just like the old homeplace, Jim. I even smell chicken. You didn't tell me. Is this the surprise?"

Her husband grinned. "No, it may be a surprise, but it's not *the* surprise. But come on now, you don't want to stand here and get knocked over. They'll be opening the gates to the public any minute now."

"Should we wait here to see it?" After all, she was here to see the grand opening.

"Nah. You see one crowd, you've seen them all. I want you to see the place before anyone else gets here." He winked. "Especially your surprise." Gently he looped her arm through his and stepped forward.

"Oh look, Jim. A blacksmith shop." Her eyes wide, she pulled away from him and walked by herself to see the brawny man with his sleeves rolled up above his elbows pounding on iron with his anvil in front of an old wooden structure. Sparks flew and Jim pulled her back a step.

She wrinkled her nose. The wonderful aroma she'd experienced had been replaced by an acrid smell. Still, the shop reminded her of long ago, so even the smell was yet welcome and somewhat familiar.

As they walked on, the rest of the family trailing behind, she stopped again, her gaze following two women clothed in long dresses that would have been in style in Branson a hundred years ago. "Why, Jim. You didn't tell me the workers wore period clothing."

"I thought you'd like the surprise," he drawled with a teasing look in his eyes.

"Oh yes. And that's my surprise. A wonderful one."

Jim chuckled, that deep laugh that still curled her toes. "Nope. That's not it."

Craft stalls lined the dirt streets of the town, and Addy took her time examining expertly handmade quilts and tatted scarves. A wood shop filled with old-fashioned, handcrafted furniture drew her attention. Over in one corner of the shop stood a horsehair chair. A pang shot through her. "Look, Jack. Your Uncle Rafe's pa used to make chairs just like this."

Jack walked over and examined the chair. "Even the bottom?"

"Of course. He made cane-bottomed ones, too. Now there's a renewed interest in caning." She ran her hand over the smooth seat. "But I don't think anyone makes horsehair chair bottoms anymore."

They strolled down to a stand where vendors made candles and displayed them for sale. Addy ran her hand down the smooth wax of short and tall tapers. The other side of the shop displayed old-fashioned oil lanterns and lamps. Some were intricately made with flowers painted on the side. She closed her eyes and allowed nostalgia to wash over her.

Jim squeezed her arm. "Just like the old days, aren't they?"

"Yes," she whispered. "Most of ours were plain, but Ma had a rose-patterned one very similar to the one on the shelf there. It's very beautiful, isn't it?"

"Yes, it is." He motioned to the middle-aged shopkeeper. He paid and asked her to wrap the purchase and have it sent to the gate to be picked up when they left.

"Thank you, darling." Addy beamed at him. "I'll cherish it always."

"And I will cherish you always." He leaned in and gave her another peck on the cheek.

She giggled. "That tickled. I think the mustache needs trimming."

"Your wish is my command," he said with a droll expression. "I trust you won't mind if I wait until later."

"I don't mind at all. But I might not let you kiss me." She wrinkled her nose.

His laughter roared across the little mountain town. "Just try to stop me."

"Now, Jim, you have me all curious. Where is my surprise?" She batted her lashes, teasing.

He shook his head. "No, no. You can't work your wiles on me, young lady."

Addy heard subdued laughter from behind them and turned to see her son and grandson shaking their heads at one another.

"Hmmph. So you don't think I'm a young lady?"

"I absolutely do, Mother," Jack said with a serious face. "You are undoubtedly the most young-at-heart lady I know."

"And don't you forget it." She smiled and gave a short nod. "All right, if I can't have my surprise, how about some of that fried chicken that's torturing me. I know it's here somewhere.

"Right this way." Jack took her other arm, and the two of them led her to a shack with a cut-out window. From inside, the tantalizing aromas of chicken and barbecued pork and beef wafted to her nostrils.

"Oh dear, now I don't know what I want. You decide, Jim." She bit her lip. "It all looks and smells so delicious."

"How about the beef on a bun?" he said. "That way, I won't have to worry about your choking on a bone while we're walking."

"Walking?" She waved toward rustic tables and chairs that sat invitingly beside the café. "Why can't we eat there?"

"Because I want to get to your surprise before the crowd finds us."

"Oh, I almost forgot the surprise. Everything is so wonderful. I'm so glad I got to come."

"I am, too. It would not have been the same for me without you here." He handed her a sandwich and then got one for himself, letting the rest of their group fend for themselves.

She took a bite and rolled her eyes with pleasure. "This is the best food I've had in years."

He laughed. "What about the fine dining we did in Paris last year?"

"No, this is better." She wiped the corner of her mouth with a paper napkin.

Jim laughed and waved to the rest of their party, who were all taking their food to the tables.

Good. She'd rather be alone with Jim.

They strolled over a bridge that crossed a creek and continued over a hill.

Suddenly she stopped, and stillness enveloped her. "Oh, Jim," she whispered.

Before her stood a small log building. A rustic sign across the door said WILDERNESS CHURCH. Except for the sign, the building looked exactly the way it had seventy years ago, when she saw it for the first time at the age of eight. But there was a deeper reason for the tears that filled her eyes and overflowed onto her cheeks.

Cupping her face in his hands, Jim brushed his thumbs across her cheeks and wiped away her tears. "And this, dearest, was your surprise."

She took his arm. "Thank you, my darling," she whispered as they walked inside.

Standing in the darkened building, Jim took her in his arms, and they shared a kiss that was every bit as wonderful as the one they'd shared when they'd been joined in marriage in that very church fifty-five years ago.

A Letter To Our Readers

Dear Reader:
In order that we might better contribute to your reading enjoyment, we would appreciate your taking a few minutes to respond to the following questions. We welcome your comments and read each form and letter we receive. When completed, please return to the following:

Fiction Editor
Heartsong Presents
PO Box 719
Uhrichsville, Ohio 44683

1. Did you enjoy reading *White River Sunrise* by Frances Devine?
   ❏ Very much! I would like to see more books by this author!
   ❏ Moderately. I would have enjoyed it more if

   _____

   _____

   _____

2. Are you a member of **Heartsong Presents**? ❏ Yes ❏ No
   If no, where did you purchase this book? _____

   _____

3. How would you rate, on a scale from 1 (poor) to 5 (superior), the cover design? _____

4. On a scale from 1 (poor) to 10 (superior), please rate the following elements.

   ____ Heroine   ____ Plot
   ____ Hero   ____ Inspirational theme
   ____ Setting   ____ Secondary characters

5. These characters were special because? _____

_____

_____

6. How has this book inspired your life? _____

_____

_____

7. What settings would you like to see covered in future
   Heartsong Presents books? _____

_____

_____

8. What are some inspirational themes you would like to see
   treated in future books? _____

_____

_____

9. Would you be interested in reading other **Heartsong
   Presents** titles? ❏ Yes ❏ No

10. Please check your age range:
    ❏ Under 18   ❏ 18-24
    ❏ 25-34   ❏ 35-45
    ❏ 46-55   ❏ Over 55

Name _____

Occupation _____

Address _____

City, State, Zip _____

E-mail _____

MAPLE NOTCH BRIDES

Party politics, parental pressure, and personal misperceptions wreak havoc in the lives of three women in historic Vermont. How will God work to make things right?

Historic, paperback, 352 pages, 5.1875" x 8"